ALSO BY MATT PRESCOTT

TEMPERANCE TRILOGY

Temperance

SHORT STORIES
OF THE WILD NORTHWEST

Outlaw's Revenge
Aces High

A THOUSAND YESTERDAYS

TEMPERANCE TRILOGY BOOK II

MATT PRESCOTT

This is a work of fiction. Names, characters, places and incidents either are the product of the author's imagination or are used fictitiously and any resemblance to actual persons, living or dead, business establishments, events or locales is entirely coincidental.

The lyrics from "Polly Wolly Doodle," by Dan Emmett. Traditional

Copyright © 2015 Matt Prescott
Tortuga Creative Group, LLC

All rights reserved.

ISBN: 1514602148
ISBN-13: 978-1514602140

For Emily
—when you're old enough to read it.

A THOUSAND YESTERDAYS

A NOTE FROM THE AUTHOR

AS STATED on the cover, this book is the second of a trilogy. Although it is possible to read *A Thousand Yesterdays* by itself and still get enjoyment out of it, doing so will diminish the impact of certain scenes and will give away the ending of *Temperance*. In other words—please read *Temperance* first. I promise you'll like it.

PROLOGUE

THE KILLER'S FACE was purple and swollen, his hands cuffed behind him. As he lifted his head to speak, a spray of blood and saliva painted the white pine wall to his right.

Marshal Whitaker's only deputy stood over the battered gunfighter, flexing and shaking out his now bloodied right hand. He reared back for another blow then stopped.

"You." He pointed to a man standing in the doorway. "Give me his gun."

"Yes sir, Mister Deputy." The man hurriedly pulled the gunfighter's ivory-handled Colt from his belt. "I was the one who took it off him. I don't know if that means I got more posse money comin' to me ..."

"It doesn't."

The deputy took the gun and examined it. Setting it to half-cock, he opened the loading gate and slowly rotated the cylinder. He turned back to the gunfighter.

"So, after emptying your weapon into five innocent men and a young boy, you stopped, not to think about what you'd done but to reload your gun?" He flipped the Colt and buried the heel into the gunfighter's temple, knocking him to the ground. "Someone pick up this piece of shit."

Lucas Kirkwood watched as two men hefted the gunfighter and placed him back in his chair. The nineteen-year-old boy had been sweeping the marshal's office when the posse brought the gunfighter in. He'd since positioned himself behind the marshal's desk and remained unnoticed throughout the deputy's beating of the killer. Now, as the deputy turned toward the desk, Lucas couldn't help but make eye contact.

"What the hell are you doing here, kid?" The deputy stepped behind the desk and stood next to the boy. He dropped the gunfighter's Colt into a drawer and slid it closed. "You like watching a no good killer get what he deserves?"

The boy stuttered, "I was j-j-just ..."

"Well, I can't blame you. I must admit, performing justice upon a murderer like this is a bit cathartic." He grasped Lucas' shoulder with his right hand, the deputy's mangled knuckles just inches from the boy's face. "You can stick around, son. Just try to stay out of the way."

As Lucas responded with a breathy "Yes, sir," the deputy returned his attention to the gunfighter who was again propped up in the chair.

"So, what do we know about our new friend here?" He punctuated the question with a swift kick to the killer's chest with his boot heel. As the gunfighter doubled over, the deputy turned to the room. "Well ... anyone?"

The man who'd handed over the killer's gun owned the livery across town. Lucas wasn't sure of his name. He was lanky, older and held a new Winchester. A couple of paces to the killer's left stood Marcus Byron who worked for the hotel. Byron was at least a foot shorter than the man in the doorway but probably weighed just as much. He rested his palms on his two holstered revolvers. Across the room, to the killer's right was Jacob Hanson, the youngest member of the posse. He held his shotgun like a man who had no idea how to use it. The double-barrels were raised and pointed in the gunfighter's general direction but shook like an aspen in the wind.

Finally, after looking back and forth to his crew, Marcus Byron spoke up.

"Sir, this here's Duke Valentine. He's a gunman that works for the cattle outfit that came through yesterday. Only know him by reputation."

"And what kind of reputation's that?" The deputy eyed Duke Valentine as he spoke to Byron.

"Well, he's a killer. Someone you definitely don't want to mess with."

"And he's fast," the man in the doorway added.

"I heard he's killed ten men." Jacob Hanson tried to steady his shotgun. "Well, I guess it's sixteen now … after what he did last night."

The deputy's full attention remained on Valentine who sat slumped in the chair at the back of the room. He took a few slow steps toward the gunfighter as he spoke.

"And how did the three of you manage to get the jump on such a seasoned killer?"

"He was just sittin' on that wagon out front." The man in the doorway thrust his thumb over his shoulder. "The one with the coffin in the back."

"We put our guns on him and told him to get down. Told him we was goin' to take him in for doin' what he did," Byron added. "He didn't resist. He didn't do nothin'. He just sat there."

"He was mumbling something about needing to bury the boy he shot." Jacob Hanson wiped his brow. "That's who's in the coffin."

The deputy took a few more steps forward. He stopped when Valentine spoke.

"You have to let me bury him." His voice was hoarse. "After that, I don't care what you do with me."

"I *have* to?" the deputy spat. "Listen here, you worthless piece of shit, I *have* to wait for the marshal to arrive, I *have* to take you to the judge in Denver and after that I *have* to watch you hang. None of those things include *having* to let you bury anyone. If it were up to me I'd beat you to death right here, right now for what you did to that boy."

The deputy took a breath and leaned in closer. "What's so important about this boy anyway?"

Duke Valentine raised his head and looked into the deputy's eyes. "He's my son."

Before the deputy could react, Valentine bolted forward, head-butting him in the jaw, sending him stumbling backwards across the room.

The gunfighter dashed to his left revealing his freed and bloody right hand, the iron cuffs hanging from his left. Reaching Byron before the men could react, Valentine pulled one of his holstered revolvers, cocked, pointed it upside-down and blew a hole out Byron's back.

As Lucas dropped behind the desk for cover he saw Valentine pivot Byron's limp body, using it as a shield against Hanson's double-barrel shotgun blasts. Byron's back exploded sending blood and flesh into the air.

Valentine shoved the mangled body aside and dove through the red mist into the room. As he slid across the floor on his left shoulder, he put a bullet into Hanson's chin that exited through the top of his head. The gunfighter then rolled onto his back and sent another bullet into the chest of the man standing in the doorway.

Making his way to a crouch, Valentine turned toward the deputy who had just regained his senses. The deputy drew his revolver just to have it blown across the room by another explosion from Valentine's gun. He raised his right hand and looked through the gaping, bloody hole the large caliber bullet had made. In shock, he eyed Valentine as another blast hit him in the belly, sending him backwards across the desk.

Valentine stood and scanned the room, his revolver landing on Lucas who pointed the ivory-handled Colt he'd pulled from the drawer.

"D-d-drop the gun, mister," Lucas stuttered. The view of the killer's gun was obscured by his own trembling revolver.

Valentine continued to point his gun at the nineteen-year-old boy.

"I m-m-mean it. I'll shoot." Lucas tried to sound threatening but knew he was failing.

After what seemed like an eternity, Valentine's shoulders sagged and he lowered his gun. He let it drop to the floor.

"I just want to bury my boy."

The gunfighter slowly turned and walked out the door.

Lucas followed him on unsure legs, never dropping Valentine's ivory-handled Colt. He fingered the trigger as the killer untied the horses and stepped up onto the wagon. Struggling to steady his hands, Lucas watched over the gun's sight as Duke Valentine rode north, leaving Durango.

PART ONE

THE MARSHAL

ONE

ZEBEDIAH CAIN STOOD over his father's dead body. The undersized pine box it had been wedged into leaned against the jail building and was propped open, he presumed, for the small North Idaho mining town to view. Black flies buzzed around what was left of his father's head, the remains of which had been shoveled up and placed next to the dusty corpse. His brother Mordecai's body lay adjacent to his father's in a slightly larger box that fit the huge cadaver perfectly due to the fact that its head and neck were completely gone. Zebediah leaned forward and rubbed the congealed blood from his father's gold badge. The word "Sheriff" soon glistened in the light as it should.

As he placed his dark bowler hat back on his head, Zebediah took a few paces down the wooden sidewalk to the last pine coffin in the row of four. The corpse inside was also missing its head but the rest of its features were very distinct. The body of his father's lead deputy, Cincinnati, was dressed in black pants and a black vest that covered what used to be a white, collared shirt. Around its neck was a thin black tie with a walnut-sized, silver pin that once held a large ruby. The crimson gem had since been replaced by a bloody hole sitting dead center.

Around the body's waist and tied to its leg was a black gun belt that held an ivory-handled Colt. Zebediah bent over, removed the revolver, opened the loading gate and rotated the cylinder. After counting five bullets, he retrieved one from Cincinnati's belt, inserted it into the only empty chamber then slid the gun behind his back and into his own belt.

He again removed his hat, grasped the solid gold cross he wore around his neck then whispered a few last words to his old acquaintance. After a moment, he placed his bowler over the mangled mess above the body's neck and stood.

Zebediah Cain was in his late thirties. He wore a sharp goatee and a thin mustache over a long face that very much resembled his father's. A shimmering, burgundy vest appointed in gold covered his off-white shirt, both of which were made of exotic fabric. Hanging low around his waist and tied to the leg of his black pants was a shiny black gun belt, much like Cincinnati's, which held a beautifully engraved Merwin Hulbert single-action revolver. Its .44 caliber, gold-plated chamber matched the solid gold rose that was inlayed into its cinnamon-colored, snakewood grips.

"Excuse me, Zeb?"

Zebediah turned to see his head of security, Beau Robarge standing with a small man he didn't recognize.

"This is Andrew Holton. He worked for Sheriff Cain. Says he knows what happened here."

Holton removed his hat, held it with both hands at his waist and lowered his head. "So sorry for your loss, Mister

Cain." Holton glanced up tentatively as if not wanting to make eye contact. "Wish I would've been here to stop this terrible thing from happening."

Zebediah took a couple of steps down to the dusty street to face Holton.

"And what exactly *did* happen here?"

Holton replaced his hat and looked up. "Well, this mountain man fella—the one who done this—had some kind of problem with Sheriff Cain and attacked him in his office this mornin'. Mordecai captured him and then Cincinnati roughed him up a bit. Then I guess he escaped and when they followed him into the street, he ..." Holton hesitated and looked at the row of coffined bodies lining the jail building. "... well, then he shot them."

Zebediah studied the small man. His hair was thin, his worn clothes dirty and his revolver rusty.

"You're telling me that this one man—this mountain man—shot my father and three of his deputies. Was it some kind of ambush?"

"No sir, I guess it was a gunfight. A showdown."

"That's impossible," Zebediah said, his tone turning harsh. "There is absolutely no way, one man gunned down Cincinnati—one of the fastest guns I've ever seen—and three other men. It just couldn't happen."

Holton backed a couple of small steps. "Sir, that's just what I heard."

"Well, you heard wrong," Zebediah snapped.

He turned to see his father's flat-brimmed burgundy hat leaning up against the base of the raised sidewalk and moved toward it.

15

"I've heard similar things from some of the miners I've talked to. They all say that only one man did this. They also say he's the same man that blew up the mine." Robarge paused, proceeding carefully. "Zeb, they say he killed Eli too."

After a long moment, Zebediah knelt down and picked up his father's hat, dusted it off then stood. He kept his back to Robarge and Holton. "Where is this mountain man? I want him brought to me." He rubbed the gold cross around his neck. "I want him alive."

Holton hesitated, then spoke. "A couple of Sheriff Cain's men headed south after him. They figured he was going down to the old way station. Guess he knows the old-timer who owns it. Don't think they was plannin' on bringing him back alive."

"Do we know anything else about this mountain man?" Zebediah placed his father's hat on his own head. It fit perfectly. "Does he have a name?"

"One of the miners in the bar across the street said he heard the name Duke Valentine." Robarge said.

Zebediah turned back toward Robarge. "Duke Valentine?"

"That's what he said. Listen Zeb, should I go after this Valentine, see if maybe I can stop the men that went after him from killing him? Bring him to you alive."

Zebediah raised his right hand and examined it. With his left thumb he rubbed the large round scar on the back then turned it over and traced the even bigger scar on the palm.

"They won't kill him."

TWO

BECKETT "DUKE" VALENTINE lay in a small bed in the back bedroom of his friend Frank Gibson's cabin. He'd collapsed there not long after he'd arrived. A gunshot wound in his shoulder, a night without sleep and the beating he'd taken from Cincinnati and the sheriff had finally caught up with him.

The room, which had belonged to Frank's daughter, Abigail, was tidy, simple and sparsely decorated with feminine touches. Below an ornate mirror next to the bed sat a small cherrywood table with a white doily covering its top. A cut-glass vase sat in its center holding two dying wildflowers. At the end of the bed and next to the door was a modest bureau with three drawers which had been emptied and left open. Beckett had placed his fourteen-inch Bowie knife in its holster-like sheath on top of the bureau as he'd entered the room then collapsed onto the bed's floral-pattern quilt.

It had only been a few hours since the gunfight in Temperance and Beckett was out cold and dead to the world. Somewhere around midday the pain from the large wound in his shoulder woke him. He drowned it with half a bottle of whiskey and since had been in and out of sleep.

Visions of Frank Gibson's dead body haunted his dreams. He'd buried his friend a hundred times in the darkness of his own head. Explosions of light had brought him half awake and then he'd fallen back to sleep and into Abigail's warm embrace. She held him in his dreams on the porch of Frank's cabin until her eyes turned to bloody sockets put there by a headless deputy Cincinnati.

Beckett bolted awake trembling and sweaty, realizing what had happened was only partly a dream. The explosions of light were now accompanied by explosions of sound pounding in his head. Quickly he realized that the pounding was coming from the front door.

His blurred vision caught a glimpse through the doorway of two figures bursting into the main room of the cabin. Immediately, instinct took over and Beckett slid out of bed and grabbed his holstered Bowie knife. With his good shoulder, Beckett lunged at the first figure as it neared his room, knocking it backward onto the floor.

As Beckett rolled to his side and slid his Bowie from its holster, the second figure struck him in the head with the stock of a rifle. The world went black for a moment, then as light slowly returned, the two figures became clear.

Two men with Winchesters stood over him. One was hefty and solid, the other—the one he'd attacked—was a half foot shorter, wiry and weak. As Beckett shook the fog from his vision, the hefty man spoke.

"Get up, asshole."

A THOUSAND YESTERDAYS

Beckett complied by immediately charging into him. The fat man was no match for Beckett's mass and fell against a table in the middle of the room, collapsing it.

Sliding his Bowie from its holster, Beckett stood and turned toward the short wiry man who was raising his rifle, his mouth agape. Beckett lunged at him, thrusting his knife into the thin man's mouth and through the back of his skull, pinning him to the wall next to the front door. The wiry man's hands clawed at the handle of the knife for a moment before his body went limp and hung twitching from the large Bowie. Blood flowed from the corners of his mouth and from the back of his head down the wall.

Before Beckett could retrieve his knife, the hefty man swung a chair at him, his wounded shoulder taking the brunt of the blow. The explosion of pain sent him stumbling out onto the porch, his right hand clutching his wound. Taking advantage of the opportunity, the fat man hit him across the back with what remained of the broken chair, toppling him down the porch steps.

Beckett collapsed into the dirt with a puff of dust, unarmed and helpless. His wounded body had finally given up. As he struggled to roll over he saw the hefty man pointing a rifle from the doorway.

"This is for Sheriff Cain."

As Beckett closed his eyes awaiting the inevitable, he heard a large blast, not from the doorway but from the barn behind him. He opened his eyes to see the fat man fall forward into the dirt at his feet. As Beckett pushed himself up, a dark pool of blood flowed from the corpse to his boots.

"Howdy, Mister Beckett," a voice said from the barn.

Beckett turned to see a thin black man with bandaged hands lower a smoking shotgun.

"Or should I call you Mister Valentine?"

THREE

ELEVEN-YEAR-OLD Samuel Baines rummaged through the top drawer of his dresser and collected a large stack of his worn dime novels. He threw the books onto his bed and frantically combing through them. Quickly studying each cover, he searched for a face he knew he'd seen before. The face of a man who was standing down the street, in front of the bank. When he finally found what he was looking for, he snuck down the stairs to his parents' store and hurried out the back.

DOC SHERMAN STUDIED the three figures through one of his saloon's two curtained windows. On the opposite side of the batwings, Harvey Coleman looked through the other. The room behind them was full of townsfolk and miners, all of whom waited for some kind of update on the situation.

"The tall one without a hat must be the sheriff's son." Harvey glanced across at Doc. "You think?"

"Must be. Looks just like him."

"Shit! I thought we'd gotten rid of them Cains." Harvey slowly pulled his large Walker Colt from its holster. "I mean, I thought Beckett had gotten rid of 'em. Completely forgot about this asshole."

Doc watched as the tall man picked up Sheriff Cain's hat and placed it on his head. "What'd you say this one's name was?"

Harvey turned to the room speaking to it as much as to Doc. "Don't remember. Just overheard some men at the mine talking about how the sheriff's eldest son was on his way here. Meanest of the bunch. Even worse than Mordecai. Guess that's him."

Seamus McCready, the town butcher, joined Harvey at his window. "Well, I know the weasel to the left is one of Cain's men. Call 'im Holman or Helmen."

Doc turned back to the window. "Holton. Comes in here and orders a rock candy and rye every morning. Says it's to settle his stomach. He rode with Reed, the one who was usin' poor Samuel Baines as a human shield earlier.

"Reed also helped Mordecai pull poor Nat's fingers off," Harvey added. "Asshole got what was comin' to him ... Reed, I mean. Not Nat"

They watched the tall man who looked like Sheriff Cain walk away from the others and into the bank.

"And who's that one?" McCready squinted. "The one armed to the teeth."

From the back of the saloon came the patter of young feet. Samuel Baines slid to a stop just in front of the batwings holding a tattered book in his hand. "I think Mister Beckett is in big trouble."

BEAU ROBARGE KICKED dust in frustration. "I don't know what to tell you. I've never seen him like this."

He and Andrew Holton stood in the street outside of the jail. They had just watched Zebediah enter the bank and head upstairs to his father's office.

"What did he mean by that? How does he know they won't kill this Valentine fella?"

"Like I said, I don't know."

Robarge took a long look around the small mining town of Temperance. The streets were mostly empty except for the occasional miner strolling into the whorehouse. A group of Sheriff Cain's remaining men milled around their horses in front of the livery a block north. The afternoon sun beat down onto the dusty earth making the street to the west disappear into shimmering trees.

Removing his flat-brimmed gambler's hat, Robarge ran his fingers through his damp dark hair. Oil and dirt covered his hand which he wiped on the back of his full-length chaps. Beau Robarge was small in stature but big in presence. His dark-skinned, chiseled jaw was lined with thick sideburns. A handlebar mustache framed his tight mouth. He'd removed his short leather coat, leaving it on the saddle of his Appaloosa and had rolled up the sleeves of his orange, wool shirt. He wore two cartridge belts over his shoulders that crossed his chest. One held twelve-gauge shells for the sawed-off shotgun holstered on his back. The other held .41 ammo for the Colt double-action Thunderer he wore cross-holstered on his left hip. The revolver's ebony grips were adorned with pearl inlayed skulls on each side.

Robarge had been riding with Zebediah Cain for over three years, working as his head of security—which basically meant he shot people when Zeb told him to. He knew what to expect from his boss's actions but knew almost nothing about his past and was both fascinated by and afraid of Zebediah Cain.

"**THAT FELLA THERE**—the one with the sawed off shotgun on his back and the Colt with the skull on it—I think he's a gunman called Robarge." Samuel caught his breath. "I've heard mention of him in some of my dime novels but never seen a picture of him. I definitely remember that skull though."

"So, you're sayin' this Robarge fella is gonna be trouble for Beckett?" Seamus McCready said. "If Cincinnati wasn't faster than 'im, I'm sure this fella won't be."

"Oh, Robarge is bad news but he ain't the trouble I'm talking about. I don't know why I didn't recognize the last name before …" Samuel thumbed through his tattered book. "See, it says right here: *There is no man meaner or more ruthless than Zebediah Cain and the only thing faster than his engraved Merwin Hulbert revolver is his vicious temper. No one alive is better than Cain with a pistol. Not Bill Hickok. Not Wyatt Earp. Not even the fabled Duke Valentine."*

Samuel looked up from his book to Doc. Then to Seamus and Harvey. They all stood quiet for a moment, comprehending.

Finally, Harvey spoke. "That's just a kid's book. It don't mean nothin'. Just a bunch of stories. Beckett can take care of him …" He waited for reassurance but none came.

"**ALRIGHT …**" Robarge replaced his hat and kicked the dust again. "I'll go talk to him."

Robarge walked across the street into the bank, up a narrow flight of stairs and into the large office above. The room was empty except for a couple of high-end chairs that faced a large desk. Zebediah sat behind the desk in an ornately carved chair that swiveled at the base, his back to the room. Pausing in the middle of the floor, Robarge waited for his boss to turn around. When he didn't, Robarge loudly cleared his throat to announce his presence. Zebediah still did not respond.

"Uh, Zeb. You mind if I have a word?"

In the quiet room, Robarge heard the strike of a match and the crackle of a cigarette being lit. A few moments later a puff of smoke rose from behind the chair.

"Have all the words you want."

Robarge again ran his fingers through his hair, scratching the back of his dry scalp. "Well, I was wondering what you wanted to do about this Valentine character. Wondered if we should go after him.

After a beat, another cloud of smoke rose into the rafters.

"I need to bury my father, my brothers and Cincinnati."

"Yes. Of course. It's just …" Robarge proceeded carefully. "… if you're right about Valentine getting the best of the sheriff's men and he goes on the run, it'll be harder to track him the longer we wait here."

"I'm not going to bury them *here*. Not in this shit hole of a town." Zebediah took another draw from his cigarette. "I'm going to take them down to that mission we passed on the way. That's what my father would want."

After another long pause and another couple of puffs of smoke, Robarge opened his mouth to speak. As he did, Zebediah spun his chair and looked him in the eye.

"I want you to take a couple of men and head down to that way station. Maybe take that one out front since he seems to know where it is. The men who went after Valentine will be dead and he will be gone. I want you to follow him."

"You still want me to bring him to you alive?"

"Yes. After I bury my father I'll come back here to finish some business then I'll ride north to White Pine. I will then take the train to our silver operation outside of Ironwood. I want you to bring him to me there."

"Colorado? I'm sorry, Zeb but that makes little sense. Why Colorado?"

A THOUSAND YESTERDAYS

Zebediah placed the remnants of a burned piece of paper on the desk. The top portion was mostly ash but the bottom third was intact.

"Because Duke Valentine is going to Durango."

FOUR

"**WHERE THE HELL** did you come from?" Beckett grunted and slowly lifted himself off the ground with his good arm.

The young black man pointed with the end of his shotgun. "From behind that stable."

Smiling, Beckett made his way onto his knees. "Well, it sure is nice to see you." He paused and took a couple of deep breaths. "It's Nat, right?"

"Yes sir, Mister Valentine. Nat Harris." Nat flipped open the shotgun and pulled out the empty cartridge, dropping it into the dust.

"Don't call me *sir* and don't call me *mister* ..." Beckett made his way up onto weak legs. "... and definitely don't call me Valentine."

Losing his balance, Beckett toppled to his left. Nat dropped his gun, hurried over and caught his arm before he fell.

"Whoa there, Beckett. Maybe you ought to sit down."

"Think you're right." Turning toward the porch steps with the help of Nat, Beckett sat on the lowest one. "Must've had too much medicine."

"Laudanum?"

"Whiskey."

Nat chuckled. "That'll do it."

He took a seat on the far side of the step from Beckett. The corpse of the hefty man lay in the dust between them.

Beckett rubbed the back of his head. "Goddamn, my head hurts."

"Whiskey'll do that too."

"So will the butt of this fella's Winchester." Beckett kicked the corpse.

From around the corner of the cabin came a low "woof" followed by a boisterous flurry of barking. A mottled gray mutt paced a few yards from them, snarling at Nat.

"So, you're going to bark at the guy who saved me, huh? Where were you when I was getting the living hell kicked out of me?"

The dog answered with a growl then barked at Nat again.

"Oh, knock it off." Beckett tossed a pebble in the dog's direction. He immediately regretted the action when pain shot through his wounded shoulder. He groaned. "You ain't scarin' nobody."

Giving a final "woof" as if to have the last word, the mutt slinked around to Nat's side of the porch.

"Who's this?" Nat held his hand out to the dog.

"Just a mutt that's been followin' me for the past few days. Well, it follows me by default when no one else better is around." Beckett though of Abigail and how she'd given the dog a name. "Guess he's called Baxter."

"You guess?"

"I didn't name him. I just feed him."

"He sure is skittish." Nat clicked his tongue.

The dog lowered its head, perked its ears and slowly inched toward him. A few steps later it reached Nat's hand, sniffed it then allowed the stranger to stroke its head.

"Told you he likes everyone better than me."

"What can I say. Dogs love me." Nat gestured toward the fresh stump on the animal's rear. "What happened to his tail?"

"Deputy Cincinnati."

"The one who killed Mrs. Sherman?" Nat turned toward Beckett. "The one you shot first?"

"That's the one. Blew it off to prove a point I guess."

Nat ceased rubbing the mutt for a moment and touched the bandaged stumps where his pinkies had been. "I know a little about that."

"Yeah, I guess you do." Beckett eyed the man next to him noticing how much the young, black piano player had changed since they'd met three days before.

The tidy, clean-cut appearance he'd had when Beckett first saw him was gone. Nat's sculpted sideburns had been neglected, his face looking as if it hadn't seen a razor in days. His white shirt, once pressed to perfection, was yellowed around the underarms, smeared with dried blood and wrinkled like an old maid's back, the sleeves rolled up above his elbows. Dirty white bandages contrasted the shiny dark skin of his hands. His two missing fingers had stopped bleeding through the dressings Doc Sherman made after the incident with Mordecai.

"How they healin' up?" Beckett nodded toward Nat's pinkies.

"Well, I don't think they'll grow back." He reached down and resumed petting Baxter.

"No. They probably won't." Beckett lifted himself off the step with a grunt.

"Whoa, now. Where are you going?" Nat stood quickly, startling the dog who jumped back.

Supporting himself against the porch railing, Beckett waved him off. "I'm fine. Just needed to rest a bit." He stepped up into the doorway and turned toward Nat. "I gotta get packed up and on the road."

NAT FOLLOWED BECKETT into the small cabin, his first step landing in a large pool of dark liquid. Just to his left hung a thin man, his head pinned to the wall with a large knife that filled his mouth. The man's front teeth had been dislodged by the knife's blow and were hanging from his bloody black gums.

"And I thought *I* was having a bad day," Nat said under his breath.

Leaning over to retrieve a saddlebag that lay beneath a collapsed table, Beckett looked over his shoulder at the hanging corpse. "You mind grabbing that knife for me?"

"This one?"

"Only if you think he's done with it."

Nat took a step closer to the dead body. "Oh, he's done with it." He grasped the elk-horn handle of the large Bowie knife with both hands and gave a quick tug. The knife didn't budge. Repositioning himself, he placed his right foot on the wall next to the body and took a deep breath. He pulled on the knife while pushing against the wall with his full strength. After a moment, it came loose and he stumbled backwards a few steps. The bloody, limp body tumbled to the floor with a thick thud.

The huge Bowie was much heavier than he'd expected. Its handle worn and comfortable, its blade sharp and covered in blood. Beckett reached out and took it from him, wiping the congealed liquid on his pants.

"Thanks."

A delayed chill ran down Nat's spine. "No problem."

"So, what *are* you doing here?" Beckett slid the Bowie into a holster-like sheath attached to a belt that he buckled around his waist. He tied a leather strap at the bottom around his thigh. "Not that I ain't glad for your help."

Nat paced around the cabin examining its contents, trying to distance himself from the dead body by the door.

"After you shot the sheriff and his men and handed me that shotgun, I did what needed to be done to that asshole who took my fingers. I stood there looking at the mess I made of his huge head for a long while, waiting for the guilt to set in. I figured taking a man's life—even a no-good man who deserved it—would weigh on my conscience." Nat took a step into a small room toward the back of the cabin. The bed had recently been slept in and looked to have belonged to a woman. "Turns out it didn't. Still hasn't. Even shooting that fella out front who was going to kill you didn't affect me."

"Bad people deserve what they got comin'." Beckett fingered through the contents of a cigar box he'd pulled from a large bag. Retrieving a piece of paper, he folded it and slid it into his shirt pocket.

"Well anyway, by the time I'd come to my senses, you'd left town and everybody was talking about you … that you were this famous gunfighter and whatnot." Nat looked into the adjacent bedroom. It was more cluttered than the first but was larger and had a longer bed. "Also remembered Doc talking about the sheriff's *other* son who was going to show up at any time. About how he was some big-shot gunfighter … kinda like you I guess."

Beckett didn't respond.

"So, I figured if this serious gunman was going to go after you, he was going to go after me too—seeing as I blew his brother's head off. After watching what you did back there I decided it was safer to follow you than it was to stick around Temperance."

Beckett set his hat on his head, winced as he carefully placed his saddlebag over his good shoulder and cinched his large tear-drop shaped pack. "Your plan is to follow me?"

"I don't know if I'd call it a plan but, yeah, that's what I had in mind. Figured we could look out for each other."

"Listen, Nat. I got stuff I need to take care of. I really do appreciate what you did back there but I don't ride with

… well, a partner. You're more than welcome to stay here in the cabin if you want. The owner ain't gonna kick you out."

Beckett took a step over the corpse in the doorway and onto the porch. As he walked into the dust toward the stable Nat yelled from the doorway.

"You're full of shit, you know that, Beckett?"

Beckett turned toward the house. "What did you say?"

"You act all tough with your big knife and your big muscles but you're just as afraid as everyone else. It may not be from men like the sheriff or his deputies but you're afraid of something."

Beckett didn't move. He seemed to be waiting for Nat to continue.

"Why won't you carry a gun? You obviously know how to use one—and that's a massive understatement. Instead, you carry that knife. You were almost killed not ten minutes ago because a fat man got the best of you with his rifle. Don't tell me you don't need a partner. You need protection as much as anyone else. You need protection from yourself, Becket!" Nat panted from his tirade. He wiped his brow and calmed himself.

Repositioning the saddlebag on his shoulder, Beckett stared into Nat's eyes. For a very long moment no words were said. The silence was broken when Beckett chuckled and smiled.

"Alright, grab your ten-gauge and come on. The trail can get pretty lonely. Might need someone to berate me now and again."

"I'm sorry about that, Beckett. I don't know what got into—"

"And grab that fat man's revolver while you're at it. At least one of us should be able to shoot."

Nat didn't hesitate. He hopped down the steps, rolled over the heavy body of the man he'd shot and removed his gun belt and revolver. As he fell into step with Beckett, the tailless mutt trailed behind him.

"Might be too late to ask but where are we going?"

"We're going to Colorado."

FIVE

FROM INSIDE SHERMAN SALOON, Samuel stood next to Doc and watched Zebediah Cain ride west along with one of the sheriff's wagons. It had been two hours since Zebediah and his partner, Robarge had arrived in Temperance.

Within the first hour, Robarge had assembled a couple of men and rode south. Afterward, Zebediah had the bodies of his father, brother and Deputy Cincinnati loaded into the wagon along with four headstones. He'd said some words to what remained of the sheriff's men and now was on his way out of town.

The sheriff's remaining men stood in front of the jail with looks of bewilderment, watching Zebediah leave.

"You think he's gone for good?" There was hope in Samuel's voice.

"No way to know for sure," Harvey said.

Doc shook his head. "They'll be back. Too much at stake here. Even with Beckett destroying one of Cain's mines, there are two more still working. That's a lot of money to walk away from."

A THOUSAND YESTERDAYS

Seamus McCready sat at the bar. He'd poured himself a large glass of whiskey and was nursing it. "You think this Zebediah character will be as oppressive as his father'?"

Doc turned to Seamus and the rest of the room. Most of the townsfolk and miners who'd been there earlier had cleared out. A few still remained. "No reason to think otherwise. If there's any truth at all to little Samuel's book here, this asshole will be worse."

"So we're back to square one …" Harvey's voice trailed off.

"Don't think we ever came to a decision 'bout what to do before Beckett came in here and took out Cain and his men," Doc said.

Seamus McCready slammed his drink down onto the bar sloshing whiskey over the lip. "Well, I'm ready to fight."

"There's only two of them." Harvey added. "We get the whole town together, we could take 'em."

A chatter of approval echoed through the room.

"I'm tired of being under them assholes' boot," said a miner toward the back.

"Me too," said another.

Doc nodded. "Alright then. We take them on." He moved behind the bar and started placing glasses onto the polished wood. "Drinks are on me, boys. Let's show these sons-of-bitches they ain't wanted."

The rest of the room cheered with approval. Harvey joined Doc at the bar and helped pour drinks.

Backing away from the celebration, Samuel sat at a table toward the rear of the saloon. He opened his dime novel to a page he'd dogeared and studied the illustration.

In the center of the picture stood a man with a marshal's badge gleaming on his vest. At his feet knelt three men facing away from him, their hands tied behind their backs. Next to them lay a body face first in the dirt. The figure with the badge towered over the three men, his revolver pressed to the head of one of them. The caption below read:

> SELF-APPOINTED MARSHAL, ZEBEDIAH CAIN DEALS OUT HIS OWN BRAND OF JUSTICE.

Samuel lowered the book to his lap and looked at the men celebrating around him. As Seamus McCready toasted the room, Samuel said to himself, "Please come back, Mister Beckett."

SIX

HE'D PULLED the charred scrap of paper from a waste basket next to his father's desk. Only the bottom third remained of what had been a letter written in black ink. Riding along side a modified conestoga wagon on his blue roan, Zebediah read the few decipherable sentences over and over to himself.

… ten years since I saw you alive, dearest Daniel. Only I can be held responsible for your sudden departure from this earth and there isn't a second that goes by that I don't wish our places reversed.

I leave today to settle my affairs in town. I will then make my way to Durango to deliver the letters I have written you.

Wherever you are, I hope you forgive me.

Sincerely and forever,
Your loving father

Zebediah looked at the jagged scar on his right hand then touched the place on his side where he still carried Duke Valentine's bullet. *Some wounds will never heal.* His eyes made their way to the three coffins in the back of the wagon. *And some wounds go deeper than a bullet.*

Folding the scrap of paper in half, Zebediah slid it into a small pocket of his vest.

He rode south paralleling the Coeur d'Alene River. A blood-red, late-September sun disappeared behind tall trees to the west through a haze of smoke. The wagon that accompanied him was once owned by his father and was used to transport ore from the mines to wherever it needed to go. Now it carried three coffins, four headstones and one grizzled old driver. The canvas top and ribs had been removed to accommodate the three stacked pine boxes.

Before he'd left Temperance, Zebediah had given the town undertaker just one hour to engrave headstones for his father, two brothers and Cincinnati. Despite the man's numerous objections to the amount of time he'd been given, Zebediah was relatively pleased with the result. Each stone was more elaborate than the last, his father's being the largest and most ostentatious.

"So you're takin' them bodies down to that fancy Injun Mission, is ya?" The crooked-backed driver spat a thick stream of tobacco across the bank and into the glassy river.

Zebediah did not respond and stroked his roan's mane. Its charcoal-blue coat shimmered in the early evening light.

The driver pressed a finger to his nose and exhaled a large wad of mucus onto the dusty road below. "Ain't never hauled corpses before. Guess there's a first time for everythin'." He scratched his head. "Nah, I take that back. There was a time back in '63 when I was haulin' these two Confederate—"

"I would prefer not to discuss it."

"Oh, sure. I understand. Emotional time." He sent another brown stream of saliva into the river. "At least these one's is fresh. Nothin' worse than a rottin'—"

"I said to shut up, old man!" Zebediah's voice boomed.

The old driver froze.

Grasping the gold cross around his neck, Zebediah closed his eyes and took a deep breath. "Listen, I'm paying you to accompany me to the Mission. Could we please stick to that and only that ... quietly?"

"Yessir." The driver turned away from Zebediah and focused on handling the reins. A moment later, he jabbed his right ear with a dirty finger, pulled out a lump of yellow wax and wiped it on his shirt. "It's gettin' kinda late. You plannin' on stoppin' for the night soon? I know a good place up ahead."

Zebediah sat back in his saddle. "We're not stopping."

SEVEN

THE SKY WAS A HELLISH crimson when Robarge exited the thick pines into a large diamond-shaped clearing about ten miles south of Temperance. Looking as if it were a glowing red eye, the sun peeked through the western tree line and bathed the clearing's soft rolling hills in a peach glow.

Behind him rode Andrew Holton on an old mare followed by another one of Sheriff Cain's men named Emanuel Quincey on a flea-bitten gray. Both men swore to have known the most direct route to the old Wells Fargo way station and it appeared they were correct.

Nestled in the center of the diamond was a small cabin next to a wood-paneled stable. Two dirt roads converged in front of the buildings, one coming from the west, the other heading south.

"That's the old man's way station." Holton pointed.

"Alright." Robarge turned his horse to face the men and lowered his voice. "We don't know if Valentine is in there or not. If he is, I don't want to take a chance on alerting him to our presence. We'll leave the horses here and head in on foot."

"You want we should all go at him from the front door?" Quincey jabbed the air with his shotgun apparently trying to illustrate.

Robarge took a deep, patient breath. "I think going blazing through the front door would be a very bad idea. That's the kind of thing that'll get us killed. If this Valentine is as dangerous as everyone including you two are saying—"

"He knocked me from a wagon when we was haulin' that ore for the sheriff," Quincey interrupted. "Got off a shot from my shotgun first but I don't think I hit him."

"I think what Mr. Robarge is trying to say is we should attack the situation a little more strategic-like." Holton nodded toward Robarge for approval.

"Yes, that's what I'm trying to say. Holton, you and Quincey check out the stable and I'll handle the cabin. We do it slowly and quietly. Got it?"

"Got it," the men said in unison.

"Good. Let's get to it."

The men dismounted and slowly crept across the valley toward the two buildings. Holton unholstered his rusty revolver and used both thumbs to cock it. Quincey scanned the horizon with his single-barrel shotgun.

As they neared the rear of the stable, Robarge signaled for the men to head around the far side. They both nodded, stepped to the building and crept with their backs against the west wall.

Robarge slid his sawed-off twelve-gauge from the holster on his back and placed his right shoulder against the rear of the stable. He carefully glanced around the east side of the building toward the front door of the cabin.

A large man lay face up in the dust below the porch steps, his chest and belly mangled from what looked like a shotgun blast. Surrounding the body was a large black stain where blood had seeped into the earth. The buzzing of flies and the smell of death turned his stomach as he took a few careful steps toward the corpse. Nearing the cabin, Robarge could see that the body's face had been torn apart. The shredded eye sockets and ripped skin were most likely the work of hungry birds.

As Robarge stepped over what remained of the large man and up the steps, the rancid smell intensified. The cabin's door squeaked on rusty hinges in the soft breeze and periodically thumped on the head of another body lying just inside its threshold. A large, congealed pool of blood blanketed the entrance of the cabin, having once flowed from the thin corpse's head wound.

Both bodies had been lying in the hot afternoon sun for hours giving Robarge the impression that no one alive had been there in quite a while. As he slid his sawed-off into the holster on his back, he heard Quincey yell from behind him.

"Ain't no horses, Robarge."

"No gear neither," Holton added.

"Valentine must be gone," Quincey concluded.

Without a response, Robarge entered the cabin, stepping over the body in the doorway. He scanned the main room, his eyes passing a splintered chair and a collapsed table. The far bedroom looked unused and plain, yet the adjacent bedroom had been slept in recently. Robarge noted that it had once been occupied by a woman.

As he turned, Holton and Quincey climbed the steps outside.

"Jesus, did you see Shaffer's head?" Quincey, bending at the waist, his hands on his knees, studied the corpse in the doorway. "Looks like someone put a sword through it."

Holton, standing behind him, went green from the statement. He turned, stepped to the porch railing and retched into the dirt.

"Hit him so hard his teeth came out." Quincey looked over his shoulder at Holton, amused at his discomfort. "See, they're laying in the blood right here."

Holton retched again. And again.

Quincey laughed. "Jeez, Drew. Get a hold of yourself. It's just a little blood."

Pushing past Quincey, Robarge exited the cabin. He crossed the dirt road to the stable and looked inside.

A minute later he returned to the point where the roads intersected and looked south. "Valentine wasn't alone."

Holton wiped his mouth and composed himself. "What do you mean he wasn't alone?"

"He was inside. These two men attacked him. There was a fight and Valentine disabled the one in the doorway. He then fell to the dirt, here." Robarge pointed at his feet then pointed at the large body in the dust a yard from him. "And then someone shot this one with a large caliber shotgun."

"How do you know it wasn't Valentine?" Quincey scratched his head. "Maybe he had a scattergun when he fell."

Robarge turned and slowly walked toward the stable. "Because there are four sets of fresh footprints around the yard, not including ours. Two sets belong to these men, one belongs to the man they attacked—who we can only assume is Valentine—and a fourth set that stood right here …" He stopped by the entrance to the stable, bent over and picked up an empty shell casing. "… and fired a ten-gauge shotgun."

Holton and Quincey looked at each other, confounded.

"They rode off as a pair to the south." Robarge paced down the road a few yards looking at hoof prints in the waning light. "It shouldn't be too hard to track them."

"We goin' after 'em now?" Holton asked.

"Right now you two are going to bury those bodies." Robarge looked at the fading pink glow to the west. "We stay here for the night."

EIGHT

BECKETT WATCHED NAT bite down and struggle to tear a off a piece of deer jerky. He chewed in an exaggerated fashion as if gnawing on tree bark.

"Sorry I don't got much else to eat." Beckett took a bite of his own over-dry jerky. "I ain't no cook so I don't carry beans with me."

Nat's jaw popped as he chewed. "Nah, it's fine. The tanned-leather flavor is bit of an acquired taste." As he swallowed, a shiver ran through his body. "I'm just working on acquiring it."

Baxter the mutt sat at Nat's feet giving him his full attention. Nat tore off another piece and fed it to the grateful animal.

"Before we get on the train in St. Regis tomorrow, I say we stop at the hotel and have a big plate of grub. I haven't had a real meal in days." Beckett rubbed his stomach. "I didn't really realize it until now."

They sat around a modest fire beneath a rock outcropping somewhere around the summit of Sohon Pass. A cold wind cut through the pines from the east and made Beckett realize he was sorely underdressed for the coming winter.

Looking down at his faded tan pants in the firelight, he could see how the last few days had played out in the stains. There were splatters of blood from the men he'd killed and the knees were dark with dirt and sweat from when he'd buried his friend Frank. His red flannel shirt had been torn and mended so many times it was almost nonexistent. The right sleeve was completely missing, torn off at the shoulder by Deputy Cincinnati, revealing the raised, heart-shaped brand on Beckett's forearm. The shirt's left shoulder had been perforated by a bullet from the same deputy's gun. He'd since gotten the wound under control but the area of the fabric around the hole was black and sticky.

As another chilly gust of wind cut through him, he was grateful he hadn't shaved his beard completely before heading into town four days earlier. The close-cropped look still kept his face shielded from the cold but the full mountain-man length he'd been accustomed to would have better suited the weather.

Crossing his arms and leaning closer to the fire, he remembered his teardrop-shaped provisions bag. Before he'd left Temperance he'd picked up some supplies from Jasper Baines at the general store. Supplies that included a new pair of long underwear.

Beckett stood slowly and walked toward his sorrel.

Swallowing his last piece of jerky, Nat shook his head at the expectant dog next to him. "Sorry, buddy, have nothing else for you."

The worn leather bag hung from a hook on Beckett's saddle. He removed it and loosened the rawhide drawstrings.

"Please tell me you just remembered you had some eggs or some bread in your pack." Nat scratched the dog who had made a grunting noise and curled up at his feet.

"Nah, just remembered I had something else to wear."

Nat, who had rolled down the sleeves of his shirt, rubbed his arms and leaned toward the fire. "Guess I forgot to bring a coat, too."

Beckett removed the dark red underwear, laid them out on a log and unbuttoned his shirt.

REALIZING BECKETT would have to get completely undressed to wear the underwear, Nat adjusted his view away from his new friend's direction not wanting him to feel uncomfortable nor himself for that matter.

"Stopping at an outfitter in St. Regis probably wouldn't be a bad idea either." Beckett removed his shirt and threw it into the fire.

In the flickering light, Nat couldn't help but notice the pattern of scars on Beckett's back and arms. The remnants of three ugly bullet wounds were distinct on his torso. Cuts and gashes were prevalent across his shoulders with a raised bit of stitching on his right bicep indicating one that had freshly healed.

Beckett's movements were slow and cautious and it was obvious he was still in a lot of pain after the beating he'd taken from Cincinnati and the sheriff earlier that day. When Nat met the six-foot-three mountain man, he'd been impressed by his size, his strength and his confidence. Three days earlier Beckett was a man in his prime. Now he seemed to be using what little strength remained to hide the fact that he was on the verge of collapse.

Catching himself as Beckett dropped his belt, Nat turned and looked into the trees in the opposite direction.

"I've never been this far east before." Nat stirred the dirt with his once-polished shoe. "Was born and raised in San Francisco. Not really used to this cold either."

"Did some work there once." Beckett grunted as he slid his arm into the long underwear. "Big place."

"Compared to Temperance it sure as hell is. Got some great musicians there, too." Nat wiggled his remaining fingers in the air as if playing an invisible piano. "That's were I learned to play."

"Never really paid much attention to music, tell you the truth." Beckett pulled his pants up and stepped closer to the fire. "Like the way *you* make it though."

"Thanks. Takes a lot of practice." Nat rubbed his bandaged hands to keep the chill from them. "My father worked for a fella who owned a fancy hotel out there. He was a good man. Let us stay in one of the rooms behind the kitchen and let me play the big grand in the parlor after the guests were asleep. That was a beautiful instrument. Really spoiled me."

Beckett fastened the buttons up the front of his long underwear. "Well, I'm sure there's plenty of pianos between here and Colorado if you plan on sticking with me."

A THOUSAND YESTERDAYS

"Don't see why not. Won't go back to San Francisco and *can't* go back to Temperance. Don't care about what's behind me anyway. Only care about my future." When they wouldn't warm, Nat slid his hands under his armpits. "Colorado sure is far. What's in Durango anyway?"

Pulling his belt around his waist, Beckett tied the holstered Bowie to his leg.

"My past."

NINE

IT WAS EARLY MORNING when Zebediah reached the Mission. He slid off his roan onto the old military road he and the wagon driver had taken from the river. A young priest dressed in a long black cassock stood on a dirt path that wound up a hill to the Mission. Next to him was a short-haired Indian dressed in a button-up shirt and pants.

"Welcome! I am Father Santoro and this is brother Longbow. What might we do to accommodate you on this glorious morning." The young priest's fingers were laced together at his waist.

"Who's in charge here?"

"Father Dinapoli is our head priest. He is partaking in morning meditation as we speak. Is there a word you'd wish me to give him?"

"I would like use of your cemetery." Zebediah led his horse past the two men and up the hill.

Father Santoro hesitated then hurried after him. "Well, um, Mister …?"

"Cain."

"Mister Cain, our cemetery is not really open to the public."

Zebediah stopped and turned toward the young priest. "Are you trying to tell me that my father and brothers are not welcome in your cemetery? Are they somehow not good enough?"

"Well, it's not that they're not good enough." Father Santoro's eyes gravitated toward Zebediah's holstered revolver. It's just ..."

"Then I'm sure you won't have a problem making room for them." Zebediah continued up the hill. "Is Father Dinapoli in the house chapel?"

"Yes, but ..."

"Good, I will speak with him there."

Father Santoro and the Indian did not follow. Zebediah could hear them frantically whispering to each other.

After a minute, Father Santoro called after him. "Mister Cain, we ask that you do not bring weapons into our house of God."

Zebediah walked on.

FATHER DINAPOLI STOOD at the parlor window of the house chapel watching a tall man lead a dark horse toward him. The man and his animal cast a long shadow across the rise, the morning sun having just crested the eastern tree line. As the man neared, Father Dinapoli saw the large revolver holstered at his hip.

Exiting the house chapel, Father Dinapoli stepped down to the grass and walked out to meet the man, his long black robe soaking up the sun's warmth in the early morning chill. A white dusting of frost blanketed the grass in the shadow of a large maple that stood outside the building. His feet quietly crunched with each step.

Within a minute the man had reached him, the dark horse's breath creating subtle clouds in the crisp air.

"Father Dinapoli, my name is Zebediah Cain."

"I know who you are."

Zebediah seemed surprised at the comment.

Father Dinapoli continued, "Your father, Walter, visits me from time to time. He speaks very highly of you. You bear a striking resemblance to him."

"You know my father?"

"Yes. He is a very devout man."

"And he mentioned me?"

"His last visit he mentioned that his son Zebediah was on his way to Idaho Territory to take over the running of his business at the mines. He is a huge supporter of our Mission."

Zebediah paused, apparently taking in the information. Finally he spoke.

"Then I suppose you won't mind if I bury him in your cemetery."

***

BY MIDDAY, FOUR HEADSTONES had been placed in the ground, three of which had bodies beneath them.

On their way into Temperance the day before, Zebediah and Robarge stopped at one of his father's mines to find it destroyed, the mine itself caved in by an explosion. After seeing his father, his brother Mordecai and his friend Cincinnati dead in town, he came to learn that his other brother Eli was deep inside that mine, tortured and burned to death behind a wall of rock.

Zebediah stood with his back to the sun in a small cemetery next to an equally small grove of aspen. The Mission of the Sacred Heart stood atop a hill in the distance like an ivory beacon. Its Spanish-style, alabaster facade glowed in the midmorning light.

Behind him and to the right, towered a large wooden cross that cast a shadow across the freshly-turned earth. A smattering of priests and Indians who lived in a small village across the rise settled in around him.

Father Dinapoli had just finished his sermon and looked at Zebediah expectantly.

"Mister Cain. Would you like to say a few words?"

Zebediah removed his father's hat and traced the brim with his thumb and forefinger. He turned it in his hand then looked up and nodded.

Father Dinapoli returned the gesture and stepped aside as Zebediah took his place above the graves. He looked down at Cincinnati's gravestone for a long moment. Eventually he spoke.

"You were one of the few men in this world I could actually trust." He pulled Cincinnati's ivory-handled Colt from behind his belt, held the cylinder to his ear and listened to its mechanism click as he cocked it. He could feel the priests tensing up around him. He slowly lowered the hammer. "I think I learned as much about gun work from you as you did from me. Wish we could have ridden together one last time, old friend."

Zebediah slid the gun back into his belt and took a step toward his brothers' gravestones.

"Eli. Mordecai. You are my brothers. You will always be my brothers." Zebediah looked up, searching the sky for words. "You were complete fuck-ups but you were family."

There was an audible gasp from one of the priests behind him. Zebediah ignored it and moved on to his father's grave whose headstone was the largest of the four. The marble obelisk rose four feet from the ground with an ornate cross sitting atop its crest. The word "CAIN" was engraved across its width.

"Father, I did it. I did everything you asked. I kept my nose clean, I kept my gun holstered and I made you money." Zebediah grasped the gold cross around his neck. "I even joined this goddamned church."

More than one gasp came this time. Father Dinapoli took a step to interrupt but Zebediah waved him off.

"Well, you know what, father. I'm done. I tried it your way and it doesn't work. I turn my back for one second and you go and get yourself killed. I love you and I respect you but I'm going to bring this Duke Valentine to justice my way. You hear me? My way!" Zebediah's voice echoed through the trees.

There was a long silence. A warm breeze cut through the aspen, their leaves applauding like a pleased audience.

Finally Zebediah moved. He took a few steps toward Father Dinapoli and spoke.

"Confessional. Now."

Father Dinapoli hesitated then nodded as Zebediah made his way up the hill toward the Mission.

* * *

ZEBEDIAH PULLED OPEN the large door to the Mission. Its cavernous wooden interior echoed with every sound. His boots boomed on the polished wood floors then reverberated off the ornately-painted ceiling.

To his left was a small pair of confessional booths. Zebediah made his way to them and knelt in the one on the right. He laced his hands on the booth's thin wooden shelf, closed his eyes and waited.

After a few minutes, he heard the Mission door open. Hurried steps echoed through the room and the curtain adjacent to him slid open. A moment later, Father Dinapoli's voice came through the intricately-carved opening.

"In the name of the Father and of the Son and of the Holy Spirit. Amen."

Zebediah remained quiet for a moment then unhooked the golden clasp around his neck. He placed the large cross that swung from it on the shelf in front of him with a hollow thud.

"Forgive me father. For I am about to sin."

TEN

THE SMALL, BLACKENED LOG gave off a faint warmth as Robarge brushed char from it with his thumb. The ash that fell mixed with his breath, visible in the crisp morning air, and gently dusted the remains of the fire.

"They let it burn out hours ago. It was small. The kind of fire an Indian would build." Brushing his blackened fingers on his chaps, Robarge turned toward Holton and Quincey. "It's the kind of fire you make if you don't want to be seen."

Quincey slumped on his horse, his eyes heavy. "They still followin' the old military road?"

Robarge walked a few paces down the slope to the east and studied the subtle path that cut through the trees below.

"Yes. I doubt they know they're being tracked. They have no reason to stray from the trail."

Holton, contorting his arm behind his back, tried to reach an itch between his shoulder blades. "You still think they're headin' to the train depot in De Borgia?"

"That or St. Regis." Robarge mounted his Appaloosa. "Don't know how far the spur has come yet."

Holton unholstered his rusty revolver and tried at the itch again. "We gonna catch up to them before they get on the train?"

Robarge pointed his horse down the trail. "We're going to try."

THE TRAIN DEPOT in St. Regis was nothing more than a large shack sitting adjacent to a set of tracks that traversed the southern edge of town. An oversized gable roof topped the building and extended five feet on all sides, covering the wooden platform that encircled the structure. Telegraph wires draped above the tracks from a pole and attached to the roof next to a stone chimney that billowed smoke into a late-morning breeze.

After dismounting, Beckett tied his sorrel to the hitch below the ticketing window and stepped onto the platform. Nat echoed his movements, looping the reins of his white mare around the freshly-carved post and accompanied him to the wooden counter.

Baxter the mutt had not followed them into town and as usual had disappeared just before they'd reached the first buildings.

The station's schedule was engraved into a wooden sign above the window.

SHORT LINE EXPRESS ... MONDAY - FRIDAY 9:45 A.M.
SHORT LINE FREIGHT ... SATURDAY 10:50 A.M.

To the right, permanently nailed to the structure was a hand-painted sign.

THE TRAIN IS 20 MINUTES LATE

Beckett looked into the small, unoccupied room behind the barred ticketing window. To the left was a pine desk with a telegraph machine sitting amidst piles of papers. To the right, pinned to the wall, were maps of the area, a calendar and a smattering of wanted posters. Beckett scanned the posters out of habit. There was no mention of Duke Valentine.

The door on the far wall was open to the rest of the structure. A warm glow radiated from inside. Above the door was a clock that showed the current time was 9:55. Beckett cleared his throat loudly trying to get the occupant's attention. There was no answer.

"Maybe you're supposed to ring for him." Nat pointed at a domed, brass bell on the counter.

Beckett tapped the bell's hammer with the palm of his hand three times in rapid succession. Immediately a man arrived in the doorway.

"The train is twenty minutes late. It's always twenty minutes late." The young station agent stepped up to the counter and pointed to his left. "Didn't you see the sign?"

"We need tickets for today's train." Becket said.

"Alright." The station agent pulled up a stool and sat. He opened a ledger on the counter below the window and held a pencil, poised to write. "Will it just be you …" He leaned forward and peered at Nat. Beckett saw the hint of disgust in the station agent's eyes. "... and your friend, here?"

"Yes. We'll also need use of the animal car for our horses."

"Well, now." The station agent closed the ledger and set it aside. "That's going to be a problem."

"Why's that?" Beckett looked at Nat.

"Only the express runs during the week. There's no livestock car on the express. There is one on the freight run but that's only here on Saturday. Saturday was two days ago." He said the last part slowly as if talking to an idiot child who didn't know how to read a calendar.

From the corner of his eye, Beckett saw Nat turn and try to conceal a chuckle.

"I'm sure Randall down at the livery would take your animals off your hands for you ..." The station agent pulled a tarnished pocket watch from his vest. "... but I doubt you'll get that taken care of before today's run has come and gone."

Beckett stepped back and caught Nat's eye. Nat shrugged. Beckett turned back to the window. "And there are no other cargo trains before Saturday?"

The station agent gave out a long sigh and pointed up. "The train schedule is plainly visible above me. I can read it to you if you—"

"Never mind." Beckett stepped away from the window and headed toward his sorrel.

"If you're going to go by horse, there is a logging road along the river that'll take you to Olive and the main

Northern Pacific run. They'll have livestock cars running daily. It's only about a day's ride north."

Beckett mounted his sorrel and turned it toward town.

ELEVEN

NAT HEARD THE TRAIN whistle echo through the streets of town as he sat at a table outside of the St. Regis Hotel. The high-pitched squeal was followed by a rumble as the morning train pulled out of the station.

"Been ten minutes since we left the depot." Nat brushed dirt and pine needles from the weathered table with the side of a bandaged hand. "Exactly twenty minutes late."

Beckett draped his saddlebag over the bench on the opposite side and sat. A night's sleep seemed to have done him some good yet he still moved slowly and carefully.

Nat looked around his feet. "What happened to the dog? Haven't seen him since we got here."

"Don't think he likes towns. Followed me like a shadow until I got to Temperance, then he disappeared ..." Beckett leaned back and made eye contact with a man inside the kitchen. "... Showed up at my side as soon as I left though."

An old man emerged from the hotel and slowly made his way to their table. His shiny bald head was surrounded by a ring of unkempt silver hair that brushed his shoulders. A long, dirty-yellow beard fell across his large belly and a stained apron draped below it.

"What can I get you boys?" The cook sniffled and wiped his red nose with a thick, dirty finger.

Beckett spoke like he'd had his order ready for days. "Half a dozen eggs, a biscuit with gravy and ham if you got it."

The cook nodded. "Salted and smoked."

"Oh, and pie. You got any pie?"

"Got a peach cobbler. Ain't got no pie."

"That'll work." Beckett turned his gaze to Nat. "How bout you? My treat. Make up for that old shoe leather you had to choke down last night."

Nat smiled and looked up at the cook. "I'll have the same." He turned back to Beckett. "Thanks."

"You fellas want some coffee too? Warm up your guts?"

"Sure." Beckett agreed. "Been so long since I had any, probably forgot what it tastes like."

"Alright. That'll be a dollar ten." The cook looked both men up and down. "Payment in advance."

Beckett placed a few coins on the table. "Keep the extra."

"Thank you kindly. I'll have that right up." Snatching the money, the cook turned and headed back inside.

Nat removed his bowler, set it on the table and ran his hand over his hair. "Think we should head north to the main line?"

"Haven't decided yet. All I know is I ain't givin' up my sorrel. Don't care how long it takes to get to Durango."

"Well, I'll leave the route up to you. Like I said, I've never been this far east. Don't even really know where Colorado is, tell you the truth."

Beckett gazed at something over Nat's shoulder. After a beat, he spoke. "Colorado is about a thousand miles southeast of where we sit. We're in Montana Territory now. Crossed over from Idaho first thing this morning." Beckett gestured toward the train depot with a nod. "If we would've gotten on the train here, we'd be headin' east to Missoula where this spur meets with the Northern Pacific which runs from Seattle to Chicago."

"That's the main line that's north of here?"

"Yup. From Missoula we would've taken it southeast to where the Northern Pacific meets the Union Pacific just outside of Butte City in Silver Bow."

"That in Colorado?"

"Nah, still Montana. After that we'd have to ride south, back through Idaho and into Utah where we'd head east to Colorado."

Nat whistled. "I had no idea it was that far."

Beckett said nothing, his attention still focused on something in the distance. Nat turned and looked over his shoulder. Cutting through the soft, pine-blanketed mountains to the west was the road they'd traveled down earlier.

***

AFTER FINISHING BREAKFAST, loading up on supplies and purchasing weather-appropriate clothing, Beckett and his new partner stood behind a butcher shop at the edge of town. While Nat haggled with a back-alley vendor over bottles of alcohol, Beckett watched the trail they'd come in on. Since they'd arrived in St. Regis, Beckett hadn't seen a single rider come down the well-worn military road. Although the chances of anyone following them were slim, he couldn't help but be cautious.

"Four bits? A bottle?" Nat said to the vendor, feigning indignity. "If I wanted to spend that I'd just go to the saloon."

"That's the best I can do, fella. Don't got much gin. These two bottles is at a premium 'cause of it."

Nat sighed. "I'll give you six bits for the two plus another four for those two bottles of whiskey."

The vendor shook his head. "This here's fine Kentucky bourbon. Ain't been watered down neither. Four bits apiece."

Nat kicked the dust and grit his teeth. He pulled some coins from his pocket and counted them. "So that's nine for the four bottles?"

The vendor scratched his head and looked up. "Um ..."

As the vendor struggled with the math, Beckett caught a glimpse of a silhouette a mile up the mountain. A few moments later the silhouette turned into a rider. Then three. All coming down the road they'd traveled.

Beckett mounted his sorrel. "Nat, we gotta go."

"Hold on a piece. I'm just about to make a deal with my new friend here."

"Now!"

Nat turned back to the vendor. "Fine. Here's ten for all four bottles." He slammed the money on the vendor's cart and grabbed the alcohol. "I hate paying full price for anything but times' a waisting."

Beckett was already on the street, heading east to the river when Nat stowed the bottles, jumped onto his mare and followed.

"What the hell is the hurry?"

"Riders."

"Shit." Nat turned and looked up the mountain. "Are you sure?"

Beckett didn't answer. He just picked up the pace, kicking his sorrel to a trot.

When they reached the river he spotted a wagon a few yards away traveling the route the station agent had suggested they take north to the main Northern Pacific line. Beckett turned and followed, being careful not to be spotted by the driver.

"Make sure you don't stray from the wagon's tracks." He looked back up the mountain. The riders were a half mile from town. "Try to stay with the hoof prints."

"How do you know they're after us? Could be anybody."

"First thing they'll do is go to the train depot. The station agent will tell them we didn't take the train and most likely headed north to the main line. We're gonna let them think that."

"Beckett," Nat said in a firm tone. "They could be anybody."

"We ain't gonna take that chance."

A few minutes later they came upon a stream that cut across the road and into the river to their right. Beckett stopped and turned in his saddle.

"We're gonna follow this to the river and then backtrack south on the other side. Don't leave the stream."

Nat nodded then followed.

Once they were safely on the other side, Beckett searched the hills for the riders. They were no longer in sight.

"Ready?" He leveled his gaze at Nat.

His partner checked his stowed bottles of alcohol, adjusted himself in the saddle and nodded. From out of the bushes came a small gray figure. Baxter trotted over and sat beneath Nat's horse, his stump stirring the dirt.

Beckett yelled, "Hi-ya!" and kicked his sorrel to a gallop.

They headed southeast away from St. Regis as fast as they could.

TWELVE

"HE'S BACK." Harvey turned from the window of Sherman Saloon to the rest of the room. "He's talking to the rest of the sheriff's men in front of the jail."

Doc hurried from behind the bar and took his place at the adjacent window. Zebediah Cain was standing on the porch below the large sign that said "Sheriff" talking to his father's men.

"Shit. It's him alright. Looks like we're gonna have to deal with that asshole after all."

"Don't matter." McCready pounded a shot of whiskey. "We're ready for 'em." He looked at Harvey then at Doc. "Right?"

"Right," Doc said, nodding at Harvey.

Harvey unholstered his large Walker Colt and sighted down the barrel. "We're ready."

"Good." McCready downed another shot. "So what'll we do?"

Doc turned back to the window. The small group of remaining miners and townsfolk crowed around.

"Well, it looks like he's giving them orders. Two of them are heading west." After a beat Doc let out a deep sigh. "And the rest are heading north. Zebediah is all by himself."

Seamus McCready picked up his Spencer rifle and joined the congregation. "What about that other fella? The one with the skull on his gun."

Harvey shook his head. "He ain't there. It's just Cain."

"Well ..." McCready pulled back the hammer on his rifle. "Let's get that son of a bitch."

Doc moved behind the bar and retrieved an old revolver, checked it and slid it behind his belt. "Harvey, head out the back and across Williams Street. Wait in the alley between the bank and the post office until I give you a signal. Seamus, head across the to the hotel and do the same."

As Harvey and McCready moved toward the back door, Doc backed his way to the batwings. "As for the rest of you. Whoever's in it with us, give us some backup ..." He stepped through the doorway. "... with whatever the fuck it is we're dong."

THIRTEEN

SAMUEL BAINES HID behind a water trough in front of his parents' store as the two men rode past him down Main Street. He vaguely recognized them as a pair of the late sheriff's thugs. One was blonde and shaggy, the other clean shaven and gray. Both were armed with revolvers and Winchesters. He studied the men until they disappeared down an alley a few buildings away.

Returning his attention to Zebediah Cain in front of the jail, Samuel watched as the ruthless killer he'd been reading about in his dime novels talked to the remaining men. Three of them had worked with the sheriff's son Mordecai as "tax collectors," shaking down the town for money. The other two looked like miners. Eventually the five well-armed men mounted their horses and rode north on Williams Street into the mountains.

Zebediah was alone in the center of the intersection, just inches from where Beckett stood the day before when he gunned down the sheriff and his deputies. There were four large, black stains in the dust around him from where the bodies had lain. A moment later he slowly walked toward the jail, climbed the steps, turned and placed his back against a pole—the same pole Deputy Cincinnati would lean against—and eyed the town. He stood with his hands in his pockets, the brim of his father's hat shielding his eyes.

On Zebediah's shimmering burgundy vest was a silver, five-pointed star that hadn't been there before. Because of the distance, Samuel couldn't read what it said but could tell its shape was identical to the one Marshal Zebediah Cain wore in his dime novel.

Samuel hurried down the sidewalk toward the jail, ducking behind barrels and horses trying to get a closer look. When he reached the alley behind Sherman Saloon he ran directly into Seamus McCready.

Seamus grabbed him by the shoulder and pulled him into the alley. "Where are you goin' boy?"

"I was just ..."

"No you're not." Seamus shot a look in Zebediah's direction. "Go home. I mean it. This ain't goin' to be good. You ain't safe."

Samuel looked down at Seamus' rifle then noticed Doc Sherman walking into the street with a revolver in his belt.

"Are you gonna take him out?"

Seamus slapped him hard on the rear. "Get outa here. I don't want you seein' this."

The boy complied and walked down through the alley toward the outhouse. As soon as Seamus' attention had returned to Zebediah, Samuel turned and slinked back to Main Street, peering around the saloon.

Doc was in the center of the intersection when he spoke. "We'd like to have a word with you."

A THOUSAND YESTERDAYS

Zebediah didn't move, his eyes still hidden by his hat.

Seamus McCready hurried across the street and stood in front of the hotel, his Spencer rifle ready.

Doc nodded to the southeast and Harvey Coleman appeared from behind the bank. He had his Walker Colt.

Soon a handful of locals and miners made their way into the street from the saloon, all of them armed.

Doc cleared his throat. "I said—"

"I heard you, Mister Sherman." Zebediah raised his head. "I just don't like your tone."

Doc hesitated a moment, looked to Harvey then to Seamus. "Don't really give a shit what you like. We want—"

"You want me to leave." Zebediah stepped down from the sidewalk into the dirt. "You want me to gather up my father's men, abandon his investments and leave your town. Is that correct?"

"Yeah. That's about it."

"And what if I don't leave? Will you, Mister McCready and Mister Coleman ..." Zebediah removed his right hand from his pocket and gestured to Seamus, then to Harvey. "... will you and all of your friends behind you just gun me down in the street?"

"If we have to." Seamus McCready raised his Spencer.

"If you have to." Zebediah gave out a short chuckle and slowly nodded. "You'll *murder* me if you have to. Well, I guess it wouldn't be the first time, now would it? It wouldn't be the first time this town rose up and murdered someone they didn't agree with."

Doc pointed at Zebediah. "Your father and his men killed a lot of good people. They *murdered* my wife. What they got was justice."

"Justice?" Zebediah turned and slowly walked toward Harvey. "My father and brothers have done some bad things but what you and your hired gunfighter did to them was not justice. That was pure vengeance."

"We didn't hire no gunfighter." Harvey raised his Walker Colt as Zebediah neared.

"You're telling me that Duke Valentine just happened to show up and kill my family?"

Doc slid the revolver from his belt and cocked the hammer. "Your father hurt Valentine just as much as he hurt the rest of us. He was just doin' what he had to."

Zebediah stopped a few feet from Harvey. "Is that the gun that Valentine used? Is that the gun that killed my father? I was told he used a Walker Colt and that you gave it to him."

Harvey steadied the large revolver with both hands.

 "You see, I was told exactly what happened here yesterday by someone who saw the whole thing. I was also told your names and your relationships to Valentine. I know just about everything there is to know about this shit hole of a town. I not only know everything about you …" Zebediah nodded past Doc down Main Street to the west. "I also know everything there is to know about who you care about."

A high-pitched scream drew everyone's attention to the shaggy blonde man who had passed Samuel earlier. He dragged a woman through the dirt, her dress torn, revealing flashes of her bare chest. She clawed at his arm and yelled for her husband.

"Seamus! Please help me."

"Louise?" Seamus McCready lowered his rifle and took a step toward his struggling wife. "Louise!"

"Don't you fucking move!" Zebediah spat, his revolver drawn and pointed at McCready. "Drop your gun or I'll let *all* of my men have a go at your lovely wife."

Seamus' voice cracked "No. Please."

"Drop it now! And stay where you are. You can have her back when we're done here."

Seamus fell to his knees, dropping his Spencer to the dirt.

The blonde man threw McCready's wife to the ground, pinning her with his foot on her ebony hair. She cried out and clawed at his ankle in vain.

"Give me the gun that killed my father." Zebediah held out his left hand to Harvey, his revolver and his gaze still on Seamus.

Harvey hesitated then opened his mouth to speak.

"I don't want your words. I want the gun. Give it to me or I'll make Mrs. McCready a lovely, newly-available widow."

Harvey stood, frozen.

"Give me the fucking gun!" Zebediah's voice boomed.

As if snapping out of a trance, Harvey stepped forward, flipped his gun and placed it in Zebediah's outstretched hand.

Zebediah cocked the large Walker Colt and pulled the trigger.

Harvey's left knee exploded in a red cloud and he fell sideways against the wall of the bank. A sharp scream quickly followed as he grasped the pulsing wound.

"Jesus. No!" Doc dropped his revolver and ran to Harvey. Sliding to a stop, he untied his apron and wrapped it around Harvey's leg. "Not again. This can't be happening again."

Zebediah lowered his Merwin Hulbert and threw Harvey's Walker Colt underneath the wooden sidewalk. It hit the foundation of the bank with a hollow thud.

"You see, Mister Sherman, I believe in justice ..." Zebediah casually slid his gun into its holster and walked toward Doc. "... not vengeance. Before I worked for my father I was a marshal ... and a very good one at that. The way I look at it, you, Mister McCready and Mister Coleman here, all conspired to murder the sheriff of this town and his deputies. All because you didn't agree with their policies."

"That's fucking bullshit and you know it," Doc spat.

"No, Mister Sherman, all I know is justice." Zebediah gestured toward the blonde man with his boot on Louise McCready's hair. "Where's the boy? I want him to see this."

A shiver of fear ran down Samuel's spine as he realized who Zebediah was talking about. Before he could run he felt a hand on his head. The fingers clasped his mop of brown hair and pulled. The gray man who had passed him earlier pulled him into the street. Samuel grabbed his wrist trying to take the strain off of his burning scalp.

"Ah, young Mister Baines." Zebediah gestured to his man. "Bring him here."

A THOUSAND YESTERDAYS

As the gray man pulled Samuel toward Zebediah, two of the miners who had exited the saloon with Doc drew their guns.

Instantly they were falling backward, Zebediah's revolver smoking from the effort. Louise McCready screamed as one of them landed at her feet. His blood splattered across her tattered dress.

The gray man placed Samuel a few feet from Zebediah.

"Leave him out of this," Doc pleaded "He's just a boy."

"My brothers were once just boys. My father was once just a boy. Even Cincinnati was once *just a boy*. So were you and your two dead friends there." Zebediah gestured toward men he'd just shot. "It didn't stop death from coming for them."

Samuel tried to be strong like Beckett yet tears escaped from his eyes. He whimpered and looked up at Zebediah who knelt down next to him. Up close Samuel could clearly read "Marshal" etched around the five-pointed star on his vest. A skull was engraved in its center.

"So I hear you and Valentine were friends." Zebediah looked south down Williams Street then west down Main Street. "Well, I have friends too."

Slowly riding in from both directions were at least fifteen men. All well-dressed and well-armed. Professionals.

"The only difference is, my friends work for the Pinkerton Agency to whom I pay a lot of money. Which means they'll do what ever the hell it is I tell them to do and they'll do it very, *very* well."

Zebediah nodded to the men coming from the south. They all had bottles of alcohol with fabric wicks. In turn, they lit the bottles, encircled Sherman Saloon and sent them crashing through the windows and into the front door. Flames quickly billowed from the openings.

"No!" Doc yelled, stumbling into the street.

"Grab him!" Zebediah gestured to Doc

A couple of the Pinkertons dismounted and grasped Doc Sherman by the arms. Zebediah leaned over and spoke directly to Samuel. "Mister Sherman is a friend of yours as well, is he not?"

Samuel's eyes glossed over.

Zebediah stood. "Did you ever have the privilege of watching my brother Mordecai pull someone's fingers off? Perhaps you saw him do it to the nigger who worked for Mister Sherman here."

Tears streamed down Samuel's cheeks.

"No? Well, it's quite a sight. Of course, he got the idea from his older brother. The only difference is, I don't like to limit myself to just the pinkies."

Another pair of Pinkertons knotted loops of rope around Doc's wrists, then mounted their horses, each one attaching a rope to their saddle horn.

"Please. No." Doc's voice was harsh.

"I'm sorry Mister Sherman. You see, you and your friends protected a known killer who gunned down five lawmen. Where I'm from that's called aiding and abetting and is punishable by death. Now, although hanging a man tends to be an adequate way to deter others from committing a similar crime, I find that removing the offender's arms is a much more effective way of laying down the law."

A THOUSAND YESTERDAYS

The two riders eased their horses forward, pulling Doc's arms away from his body, lifting him off the ground. Samuel heard the muted pop of one of his shoulders coming out of its socket. A long scream followed.

"And don't think I've forgotten about your two sons," Zebediah said into Doc's ear. "The rest of my men are on their way to your newly acquired gold claim to question them as well. Hopefully they had nothing to do with your friend Valentine."

Doc struggled against the ropes causing one of the horses to step forward, popping his other arm out of its socket. He let out a scream and closed his eyes in agony.

"You see, Mister Baines ..." Zebediah quietly spoke to Samuel. "This is what happens when you befriend someone like Duke Valentine."

Zebediah stood and addressed the town. His voice echoed through the streets.

"My father owned this town and you killed him. Now Temperance is mine. I am going to find your friend Duke Valentine and I am going to punish him. I will then return and mine these hills for all they're worth. Until then, I'll leave my best men here. If when I return, anything is out of place, I will hunt each and every one of you down and give you what you deserve." He walked over and looked Doc in the eyes. "Just like our friend here."

Sherman Saloon was now completely engulfed in flames sending thick black smoke billowing into the sky. The upstairs windows burst from the heat sending glass showering down to the dirt. With each explosion, the two horses tied to Doc's arms became more nervous, tightening the ropes.

Zebediah cocked his revolver, pointed it to the sky and pulled the trigger.

The two startled horses reared and took off in opposite directions.

PART TWO

THE BOUNTY HUNTER

FOURTEEN

THE FAMILIAR TASTE OF BLOOD slowly overtook the metallic flavor of the pistol in his mouth. Garrett Stilwell knelt on the rough and muddy trail, his head forced back. The tears that burned the corners of his eyes were not caused by pain but by paralyzing fear. The front sight of the road agent's rusty Smith & Wesson had shred the roof of his mouth as it was forced between his jaws. The clicks of the hammer being pulled back reverberated through his teeth and skull and stung his ears.

"You'd better get your hands off me, boy."

As a reflex, Garrett had grasped the dirty man's forearm above the hand that held the gun. He immediately dropped his hands to his side then swallowed. The thick, salty liquid that coated his throat almost made him gag.

"Where is she?" The dirty man's voice was ragged.

When Garrett didn't answer, the man removed the gun from his mouth and cracked him across the temple with its hard grip. The world went dark for a few seconds as Garrett fell to the ground. He came to when he felt a warmth flow across his leg. The smell of urine followed.

The fat man behind the wagon stopped rifling through Garrett's belongings long enough to observe, "Shit, Levi. You made him piss himself."

The Mexican inside Garrett's wagon continued to throw cargo out onto the trail.

"We know you got a woman with you—unless these knickers are yours ..." The dirty man laughed.

The others joined him.

At the dirty man's feet was an open, canvas bag. He bent over, grabbed a handful of shimmering fabric and held it to his nose. Inhaling deeply, a smile crossed his lips. "Nope, these can't be yours. Only a fresh cherry's been in these." The dirty man leveled his revolver at Garrett. "Tell me where she is. I promise me and my boys will play nice."

As Garrett pushed himself off the ground he repeated in his head: *Don't look toward the bushes. If you look toward the bushes they'll know she's there.* He willed his eyes to stay on the wet and rocky trail.

"We're gonna find her eventually. If you save us the trouble and tell me now, I promise I won't kill you. Might not even make you watch."

Without moving his eyes, Garrett focused on the thick wall of black hawthorn to his left. With his peripheral vision he could barely make out the small figure hunched in the darkness. Even though they'd only just met, he was terrified for her. Almost as much as he was for himself.

***

TWENTY-FOUR HOURS EARLIER, Garrett sat in a rickety chair toward the back of a dark saloon in the heart of Helena. A dirty glass of gin lay on the table in front of him. Every time he took a sip, he was reminded how much he disliked the clear liquid. Not being a fan of whiskey either, he thought he'd give the juniper-infused liquor another shot. Next time he'd just order water.

Garrett was small, thin and though he'd be twenty-nine in the spring, looked as if he were just a few years out of school. A tan duster covered his worn clothes and he carried a short-barreled Remington across his belly. The gun was mostly for show which was good because he barely knew how to use it.

He had come to Montana Territory earlier that year for work when he was told the local shipping depot was looking for drivers. Not being one for hard labor, he figured sitting on a wagon all day seemed like a job he could handle. As it turned out, he was right. At first he made a bi-monthly trip north to Fort Benton and was well paid. Enough so that he was able to purchase his own wagon and eventually contract out his services to multiple companies. He enjoyed being his own boss almost as much as he enjoyed the beautiful open spaces between towns.

As he relaxed in his chair eyeing the scantly-dressed whores huddled near the stairs, he felt a shiver run up his spine, making the hair on his neck stand erect. A cold, late-September breeze poured in from the front door drawing his attention to the figure standing in the opening. As the girl entered, he was instantly mesmerized.

Her skin was aglow, her features were soft and her hair looked as if it were on fire. A light-colored dress clung to her subtle curves but instead of an overcoat she wore a thick fur vest made of what looked like black bear. She sauntered over to the bar, her hips swinging like a pendulum. As she leaned over the polished wood to engage the bartender, Garrett's eyes followed her curves the rest of the way down.

"Holy God, would you look at that?" A man standing to Garrett's right leaned toward him. "You ever seen anything like her?"

Garrett contemplated the question. "Don't reckon I have."

Halfway through the statement, his heart stopped. The bartender's finger pointed her in Garrett's direction and their gaze met. Her eyes were a shade of green he'd never seen before. He felt an acidic sting rise in his throat as she made a beeline to him. The man to his right backed off toward the bar.

"You the fella who drives the wagon out front?" Her voice was even sweeter than he'd expected.

Garrett swallowed the bile in his throat. "Y-yes, I am."

She dropped a canvas bag on the floor with a thud, pulled out the chair across from him and sat down.

"I hear that you are a private contractor … that you can make special deliveries."

"Sure." Garrett wiped his brow and sat up, trying to compose himself. "I'm here to service you—" He cringed at his words and swallowed again. "I mean, I'm at your service."

A subtle smile crossed her lips. "Good. Then I have a job for you. Are you available today?"

"Today?"

"Yes. Right now, actually."

"Uh ..." Garrett looked around the room for support. Remembering he was on his own, he turned back to her. "Yeah, I'm available."

"Great!" She sat back in her chair, pleased.

Garrett paused for a second then came to his senses. "Where exactly did you need me to go?"

"Radersburgh" Her tone was matter-of-fact.

He nodded then looked at her quizzically. "Why, exactly?"

She reached inside her dark black vest, removed a fold of banknotes an inch thick and slammed it on the table. "That's why."

FIFTEEN

HE DIDN'T ASK about the cargo she'd had him load into his covered wagon and honestly he didn't care. She had been sitting next to him for the last six hours and he was still in a haze of wonderment. Other than the large crate in the back, she carried only two bags. The heavy canvas one she'd brought into the saloon was in the back with the rest of his supplies and at her feet was a long leather pack that had been tied to her mare. Garrett assumed it must contain a parasol or umbrella.

Their conversations had been brief and for most of the trip she seemed to be in a different world. Periodically he would steal a sideways glance at her bouncing on the bench next to him. Its squeaky springs were in need of replacing causing it to bound in an exaggerated fashion. Normally this got on Garrett's nerves but today, he didn't mind it.

Finally, an hour or so before dusk, she spoke.

"When were you planning on stopping?"

"Didn't know if you wanted me to. You're the boss on this trip."

"Well, I figure we gotta eat."

His eyes flashed in her direction. Her legs were crossed toward him, a warm smile on her face. He worked the skid break to slow the wagon. "I figure you're probably right."

After building a fire and setting up camp, Garrett filled a pot with water and untied a bag of beans.

"I ain't so good at cookin'. If you was hopin' for a good meal, you are welcome to take over." He motioned to her with the pot.

"Ain't much of a cook myself. Manage to make oats taste like liver most of the time. I'm sure you'll do fine."

He nodded and dropped a couple of handfuls of beans into the steaming water.

They sat in silence for the better part of an hour when finally, Garrett opened his mouth. "That's a beautiful palomino you got there." He gestured toward the golden mare tied to the back of the wagon. "Ain't never seen one like it."

"Belonged to my mother." Her voice seemed to catch for a moment. "Gave it to me last year."

He stirred the dirt with his heel desperately searching for a segue. As he did, a drop of cold rain landed on his nose. He looked up to see total blackness.

"Looks like rain." He filled a bowl with beans and handed it to her. "Where was you plannin' on sleepin'?" His tone was hopeful.

She took the bowl and blew the steam off of it. "Under the wagon."

The rain slowly dampened his shoulders. He hesitated for a beat then eyed her. "That's usually where I sleep."

She looked at him through the steam. "Not tonight."

***

GARRETT WOKE to the smell of something being fried in grease. The large pine he lay beneath had shielded him from the majority of the night's downpour yet he was still soaking wet and shivering. He sat up to see the girl kneeling over a small, smoky fire holding a simmering pan. She'd wrapped the handle in fabric to protect her hand from the heat.

"I felt bad about you sleeping out in the rain so I thought I'd make you breakfast." She poked at the contents of the pan with a fork. "Found some eggs in the back. Figured I couldn't ruin them too bad."

Garrett threw aside his heavy, damp blanket, stood and removed his duster. He balled it up and squeezed a steady stream of water onto the ground.

"It smells great, Miss … you know, I don't think I ever got your name."

The upward curve of her soft lips disappeared. "Names ain't really part of the deal." She looked him in the eye. "Just transportation."

His face flushed as he shook out his coat. "Sorry. I didn't mean—"

"Don't be." She picked up a tin plate, slid the eggs into it, stood and handed it to him. "It ain't nothin' personal." Her smile returned as he took the plate.

"Well, I surely do appreciate a warm breakfast. Don't usually treat myself to 'em." He shoveled in a mouthful.

The eggs were charred and greasy and crunchy from bits of shell.

She eyed him waiting for a response.

He hesitated, swallowed without chewing hoping it would stay down and gave her a big toothed grin. "They're good."

"See, even *I* can't mess up eggs."

He finished off the plate as quickly as he could, pouring the remaining char and grease onto the dirt. "As soon as I get packed up we can move out."

"That would be great. Thanks."

"Garrett," he said. "You can call me Garrett."

She paused, seemed to think for a moment then nodded. "Thanks, Garrett."

SIXTEEN

SHE KNELT on the wet ground behind the strand of black hawthorne watching Garrett get beat down by the road agent.

Her traveling companion had noticed the three men riding up on them just as they'd crested the rise. Garrett had told her to jump down and hide and that he would take care of them. She'd seen the small Remington on his belt and figured he knew how to use it. Grabbing the leather pack at her feet before jumping, she hurried and crouched behind the thick bushes all the time wishing she had her canvas bag instead.

Quickly she'd realized Garrett was not a man who could stand up for himself. The lead road agent had pulled him from his place on the wagon, removed his Remington and had thrown it aside before Garrett could react.

Now it looked as if the lead man might just put a bullet in poor Garrett's brain. She moved to unwrap her long leather pack when the Mexican inside the wagon yelled out.

"Señor Levi. He's got some big crate back here."

A THOUSAND YESTERDAYS

The man he called Levi—the one with his gun to Garrett's head—turned toward his compadres.

"What kind of crate?"

"Don't know, but it's huge."

"Well then, open it up." Levi turned to Garrett. "You got somethin' valuable in there? You runnin' guns or sometnin'?"

Garrett kept his eyes on the road.

"It's nailed shut!" the Mexican yelled.

"Jesus Christ." Levi rolled his eyes. "Then get the goddamned pry bar."

The fat man made his way to one of the horses, removed a metal bar from the saddle, then handed it to the Mexican. As he slid it under the lid of the crate, she stood.

"You with the Schofield—drop it! You other two—back away from the wagon!" Her voice was loud and firm. Turning toward Levi, she pointed the Henry rifle she'd pulled from her leather pack. "I said drop it!"

Levi hesitated a moment then looked to his men. "Well, would you look at this." He eyed her up and down then turned to Garrett." This is what you was hidin' from us?"

She fired a shot that landed at Levi's feet then quickly cocked the rifle and pointed it at his head.

"Whoa now, girl." He threw his old Smith & Wesson aside. "No need for that."

She swung the barrel toward the other two men who'd backed away from the wagon. "You, too. Drop 'em."

The men looked to Levi. Neither of them moved.

"I'm serious. Drop them guns!"

"We don't mean you no harm, señorita." The Mexican said.

"Yeah, we just want to be friendly." The fat man laughed. "Why don't you come over here and we'll show you."

She was about to respond when she heard Garrett's voice. "Look out!"

As she turned, Levi fired a Derringer he'd pulled from his pocket. The bullet hit a rock to her left. Instinctively, she pulled the trigger and hit him in the chest. Blood sprayed out from behind him and he fell hard to the damp trail.

She cocked and turned toward the other two men.

The fat man pulled his gun. She shot him through the heart and he fell against the wagon. Blood trailed him to the ground.

She cocked again and hit the Mexican in the head as he pulled the trigger on his pistol. He fell backwards, his gun going off harmlessly away from her.

Levi struggled, choking on his own blood. Cocking her Henry, she stood over him. He mouthed silent words for a moment, then convulsed and finally went limp. A large pool of dark blood was already forming around him.

"You got 'em." Garrett had lifted himself up and was standing behind her. "I can't believe you got 'em."

She lowered the barrel of her rifle. "I can't believe it either."

"You took them boys out like a pro."

"I ain't no pro." She looked at the other two dead men. "Ain't never killed a man before."

"Well, you sure did a good job killin' them three.

A THOUSAND YESTERDAYS

She looked at Garrett through the black powder smoke. He was pale, his eyes were swollen and a trickle of blood escaped from the corner of his mouth. Suddenly she noticed her left hand burning on the hot, exposed barrel of the Henry. She dropped it and flicked away the pain.

"I thought I was dead." Garrett made his way toward her. "And I thought ... Well, I thought they was gonna do worse to you. You're amazing with that rifle."

Bending over her canvas bag, she tore through it. She removed a leather belt with two holsters that held matching pearl-handled Colts. She wrapped it around her hips and buckled it.

"Must've been lucky. Never really use a rifle." She removed one of the revolvers, spun it then re-holstered it. "Better with my Colts."

***

AFTER BURYING THE BODIES at Garrett's insistence and loading up their gear, they made their way back along the trail to Radersburgh. The sky was dark and threatened moisture but none came. A cold wind billowed from the north, forcing her to pull her bearskin vest tight, reminding her that winter was on its way.

Just before sundown, she turned to Garrett. "My mother's in that crate." She paused, composed herself then continued. "Left her a few months ago to help my father in Idaho. She died of an infection two days before I returned home. Need to take her to the family plot in Radersburgh."

After a beat, Garrett opened his mouth. "I'm very sorry for your loss."

"Don't be. Wasn't your fault. If anything, it was God's fault but we can't blame him now can we?"

Garrett didn't answer.

"It's just the way things got to be I guess." She looked off into the distance for a moment. "Never thanked you for standing up for me back there."

He looked at her quizzically.

"You know, not giving me up to those men."

Garrett nodded. "No problem. It was somethin' any gentleman would do."

"No, it was more than that … and I thank you." She gave him a warm smile.

"Well, you're very welcome."

After a pause she said, "Abigail."

He looked over at her.

"You can call me Abigail."

SEVENTEEN

CLAYTON FITZSIMMONS looked up from compositing his weekly newspaper to see the well-dressed marshal enter his office. Placing the final two letters of a sentence into the plate, he wiped the residual ink from his stained hands on his apron and smiled.

"Howdy, Marshal. What can I do for you?"

"I'm looking for the sheriff." The marshal gestured to a stenciled window next to the door that read:

WHITE PINE GAZETTE AND SHERIFF'S OFFICE

"You're lookin' at him." Clayton pulled aside the denim apron from his chest, revealing a tarnished badge. He removed his wire-rimmed glasses and held out a hand to the marshal. "Sheriff Clayton Fitzsimmons at your service."

Ignoring the gesture, the marshal turned and walked to the large printing press across the room. "You're the sheriff *and* the newspaperman?"

Clayton awkwardly retrieved his hand, ran it through his thinning hair and joined the marshal. "Sheriff, reporter, printer … I'm whatever the town needs me to be. I distribute the Gazette as far west as Spokane and as far east as Missoula. Kind of exciting being in the middle of the action really."

The marshal smoothed his hand over the curved, metal arm of the press. "Can you print posters as well?"

"Sure. Can print just about anything."

"And can you distribute them?"

"Like I said, as far west as Spokane, as far east as Missoula. Get them all the way to Chicago if need be. With the train running twice a day now, I can get them just about anywhere."

"I would like to put out a warrant."

"Really?" Clayton struggled to keep the elation from his voice. "A warrant on whom?"

The marshal paced back to the doorway. "In your records as sheriff, do you have any info on a killer named Duke Valentine?"

"Duke Valentine?" Clayton let out a short giggle. Pausing to compose himself, he hurried to his desk, pulled open a drawer and rifled through some papers. "Duke Valentine, the man with the brand? Duke Valentine, the best and deadliest gun in the west?" Clayton quickly leafed through a stack then tossed them to the floor. After pulling open a second drawer he finally found what he was looking for. "Ah ha!" He held the yellowed piece of paper to the light. "Duke Valentine …" Spinning the paper, he slid it across the desk. "The killer who disappeared."

A THOUSAND YESTERDAYS

ZEBEDIAH MOVED to the newspaperman, picked up the worn poster and studied it.

REWARD
($1000)
FOR THE CAPTURE, DEAD OR ALIVE OF ONE
DUKE VALENTINE
AGE, 25-30. HEIGHT, 6 FEET 3 INCHES. WEIGHT, 200 LBS.
BROWN HAIR, EVEN FEATURES. HAS A HEART-SHAPED
BRAND ON LOWER RIGHT ARM.
HE GUNNED DOWN MORE THAN EIGHT INNOCENT MEN
AND ONE YOUNG BOY IN COLD BLOOD.
THE ABOVE REWARD WILL BE PAID FOR HIS CAPTURE OR
POSITIVE PROOF OF HIS DEATH

JOHN WHITAKER—MARSHAL
DURANGO, COLORADO TERRITORY

The words were accompanied by a sketch of Valentine's face. It only vaguely resembled the man who had put the hole in Zebediah's hand a decade earlier. He placed the paper back on the desk.

"Picked that piece up ten years ago when I was a deputy in Arizona." Clayton Fitzsimmons retrieved the poster and examined it as if it were precious. "It's the prize of my collection. Even more rare than my Jesse James."

"I would like to put out a warrant for his arrest."

"You've seen him? You've seen Duke Valentine?"

"I would like posters made. I want him *alive*. There will be no reward if he's dead. And I want him brought to me in Colorado. A town called Ironwood."

"Sure." Hurrying to the printing plate he'd been working on earlier, Fitzsimmons dumped the contents onto the ground and selected new type. "And to whom shall I say he should be delivered?"

"Marshal Zebediah Cain."

Fitzsimmons stopped what he was doing, his eyes went wide and his jaw dropped. After a beat he squeaked out, "Holy shit. I don't believe it."

"How soon do you think you can get them out?"

"I'll get started right away. The posters will be done and on the next train in a couple of hours. Should be half way to Denver in a couple of days."

Zebediah rubbed his neck in frustration.

"Of course, if you want to get the word out faster, I also run the telegraph." Fitzsimmons gestured to a machine in the adjacent room. "Have the warrant out to half the country by the end of the day."

Smiling, Zebediah nodded. "Yes. That would be perfect." He slid a roll of cash from his pocket and placed it on the desk, turned and walked toward the door.

"Marshal Cain." Fitzsimmons followed. "You didn't say what the reward money would be. Do you want to stick with the original one thousand dollars?"

Zebediah paused in the doorway, tracing the scar on his hand.

"Make it ten thousand."

EIGHTEEN

WRAPPING HIMSELF in his thick new overcoat, Nat tried to forget about the blustery wind chilling his bones from the east by throwing a gnarled stick for Baxter. The mutt dashed after it, stopped a foot away then pounced. After tossing the stick in the air and chasing it for a while, the dog brought it back, dropped it at Nat's feet and waited, tongue flapping, stump wagging. Bending over, Nat picked up the stick and threw it a few yards down the far side of the rise. Baxter tore off after it.

Another frigid gust cut through the trees and hit him in the face, paralyzing him for a moment. After shaking it off, he flipped up the collar of his coat, sat on a log and covered as much of his body as he could with the long, dark fabric.

Beckett knelt on the ridge behind him, facing west. From where he sat he had a clear view of the valley they'd traveled earlier that afternoon. He hadn't moved in at least twenty minutes. The clothes Beckett had purchased the day before looked almost the same as the torn and bloody ones he'd thrown away, only now he wore a thick, sheepskin coat over them. The cold wind didn't seem to bother him, or at least he was doing an amazing job of hiding it.

"We haven't seen hide nor hair of them for over a day." Nat bent over, picked up the stick Baxter had just delivered and tossed it. "Don't see how one of your Indian fires would give us away even if they were—being all the way up here on a ridge in the trees and all."

Beckett didn't move. He was like a gargoyle poised on the roof of a church.

"Hell, we don't even know if they were really after us anyway." Nat pulled his small bowler down as far as he could but it only covered the very tops of his ears. "Probably just some loggers heading into town for a poke."

Beckett placed his hand on his hat to keep it from flying away as another strong gust blew across the ridge.

After throwing the stick again, Nat sighed, stood and walked to his mare. He pulled one of the bottles of gin from his saddlebag and popped the cork. "Can we at least set up camp? Wrapping up in a dirty, old saddle blanket doesn't sound all that bad right now."

Still no answer.

"Fine. No fire, no camp. I get it." Nat took a long pull from the bottle. The gin had definitely been watered down. He no longer felt guilty about swindling the merchant.

Nat moved to where Beckett was crouched, sat on the cold, shale ground and leaned with his back against a rock wall. He held out the bottle to his partner who said "no" with a subtle shake of his head.

Baxter trotted over and flopped down at Nat's feet, furiously gnawing on the stick.

A THOUSAND YESTERDAYS

"You haven't said but two words since yesterday. Pretty sure talking isn't going to alert anyone to our whereabouts." Nat was beginning to believe that Beckett had made a game of not speaking. As if he were trying to drive him crazy.

He took another swig of the watered-down gin. Then he had an idea. "Who's the girl?"

Beckett's face broke like a statue slowly coming to life. His shoulders lowered and he turned to look at Nat. "What?"

"The room you were staying in ... back at the way station. If I'm not mistaken, that was a woman's room. Who is she?"

Beckett turned back to the valley. "Nobody."

"Nah. Had to be somebody. Why'd you pick that room to sleep in? Other one was way bigger. Bigger bed. Better for a big man like yourself. Was she your—"

"Her father was one of my oldest friends."

"He the old man that owns the place?"

"Until Cincinnati shot him."

"Oh." Nat took another drink. He hesitated to push the subject any further.

After a beat Beckett continued. "She was staying with him. Came up from Montana to help out after his accident. Sheriff Cain wanted his land so Cincinnati killed him. Shot her twice while he was at it. Her name's Abby ... Abigail."

"Cincinnati shot her?"

"Across the arms." Beckett ran a finger along each arm just below the shoulder. Then he pointed at the dog. "'Bout the same time he blew your friend's tail off."

Baxter looked up from the stick, ears perked, stump wagging.

Nat leaned over to pet the mutt. "And that's why you came back to Temperance to kill Cincinnati. Makes sense now. He deserved what he got after shooting an old man and a helpless woman."

"Abigail is far from helpless." Beckett adjusted his pose, both knees cracking like firewood, then leaned against the rock wall next to Nat. His attention shifted away from the valley below. "One of the fastest guns I've ever seen. She carries a pair of double-action Colts and can empty them quicker that most folks can draw. Just not quite as fast as Cincinnati."

"And Cincinnati wasn't quite as fast as you."

Beckett gave him a knowing glance. "She ain't no killer though. She was lucky he only winged her. Could've done much worse."

"It's a rare thing—a woman knowing how to shoot. She have a man back in Montana?"

"Don't think so. Said she ain't one for marriage."

Nat turned the bottle on his knee. "Were you and her—"

"She moved on." Beckett lifted himself up, resuming his position on the ridge. "Just like I did."

Nat took another draw. The liquid was warming him from the inside. He'd almost completely forgotten about the freezing wind. "I had a girl once. Back in California. She was a cook at the hotel. Made the best damn grits you ever had. Loads of butter. Thought about marrying her before I left town. Never really—"

Beckett's hand went up in a gesture that said, "wait." He hopped to his feet and slid a few yards down the ridge, stopping behind a thick pine.

"What are you doing?"

A moment later Beckett hurried back up the rise past Nat and to his horse. "It's them."

Nat looked across the valley. He saw nothing but tall grass undulating in the breeze. "It's who? Beckett there's nobody—" Then he saw them. Three figures on horseback exiting the tree line a mile away.

"Oh, shit!"

NINETEEN

GARRETT AND ABIGAIL arrived in Radersburgh a few hours before sundown via a well traveled stagecoach road. Not many words had been exchanged since their run-in with the road agents that morning. Even though Garrett was desperate to discuss it, he could tell Abigail preferred—possibly even needed the silence.

Angry clouds had been following them all day and finally let loose as they reached the undertaker's office. Thick curtains of rain swept the wide dirt streets, instantly forming streams in every rut and crack. Within minutes a small river cut through the center of town.

Garrett kept out of the way as Abigail made arrangements with the undertaker and the local priest. He spent most of the time standing beneath the overhang out front, watching the storm work its way out. The downpour had almost completely ceased when the priest pulled alongside his wagon with a shiny, black-curtained hearse.

After helping two Chinamen unload the crate with Abigail's mother's remains from his wagon to the next, he took a place beside her on the sidewalk, reluctantly awaiting his imminent dismissal. Although he'd prefer it to continue, their business relationship was completed. He had upheld his end of the bargain.

"Garrett?" Abigail's sweet voice cracked.

He sighed, his shoulders dropping. "Yes?"

"Would you mind—"

"Not a problem." Tipping his hat, he stepped down into the mud toward his wagon. "I'll just get on the road."

"No, wait."

Garrett stopped and turned back.

"I meant, would you mind goin' with me to the cemetery? Don't really know anyone here. Be nice to have a friend with me"

Garrett's heart kicked in his chest. He couldn't keep the large smile from overtaking his mouth.

"Uh, sure. Sure. No problem." As he stepped back onto the sidewalk he stumbled on a seam and came to an awkward stop. "I can stay. You know, if it'll help."

A smile crossed her lips followed by a soft chuckle. Her glossy green eyes brightened. "Yeah, it'll help."

***

HER MOTHER'S GRAVE was within the boundaries of a low, wrought iron fence that encircled their family's plot. The headstone sat to the left of Abigail's grandparents and in front of her uncle and the graves of his family. He, his wife and four children had died in a fire the year before. Their headstones spanned the full southern boundary of the plot.

Abigail watched a pair of Chinamen fill in her mother's grave with shovelfuls of dirt and mud as the priest spoke. He'd only gotten a few words into his sermon when she interrupted, reminding him that she wished it to be brief. He conceded and said, "Mary Elizabeth Amelia Gibson, may God rest your soul." As soon as he was finished, Abigail turned and walked back into town. She could hear Garrett's hurried footsteps in the mud behind her.

When they reached Garrett's wagon, she stopped and looked at the sky. The dark clouds that followed them all day had dissipated to the west, leaving blue sky behind. The sun had begun its retreat behind the western tree line. She guessed it was around six o'clock. Too late to get back on the road.

She turned toward Garrett. "You hungry?"

He hesitated as if shocked by the question. "I guess I could eat."

"Thinkin' about heading over to the hotel for some food. Wanna join me?"

"Sure." There was obvious glee in his voice.

Abigail led Garrett across the street and into the Patterson Hotel where they sat across from each other at a small table in the corner of the parlor. On the outside, the hotel was old and weathered. On the inside though, everything looked brand new. The freshly-applied wallpaper's subtle acrid aroma somehow complemented the strong smell of the recently-lacquered table and chairs. The floors were well-worn but had been mopped and polished. Even the large windows that faced the street appeared to have just been cleaned.

A well-dressed desk clerk who looked to be in his late teens greeted them. She could feel his eyes travel down her figure and land on her holstered Colts. After some general pleasantries, he took their orders then disappeared into the kitchen. A few minutes later he brought Garrett a steak with gravy and Abigail a bowl of beef stew and cornbread.

"That was a very nice sermon." Garrett carefully and methodically cut his steak into small, bitesized pieces.

"Only asked the preacher to be there because that's what my mother would've wanted." She sipped a spoonful of the lukewarm stew. "Figured she can't hear him talk so why should we have to sit through his blabbering."

Garrett opened his mouth to speak then apparently decided against it. He instead shoveled in a forkful of meat.

"I really do appreciate you bein' there with me. I know funerals ain't fun."

"Uh, happy to do it."

She took another spoonful. The stew was pretty good. Better than she could make. As she looked around the room she caught the desk clerk studying them from behind his podium. When she made eye contact he quickly looked away.

"Excuse me." Abigail raised her hand to signal the well-dressed clerk.

He straightened his vest and slowly walked toward them. She could see his cheeks flush as he approached. "Yes, miss?"

Abigail leaned across the table, laced the tips of her fingers and gave him a curious look. "You wouldn't by any chance have any chocolate back there would you?" She turned to Garrett and looked him in the eye. "It seems like years since I had any. Feel I deserve it."

"I'm sorry, miss but I'm pretty sure we don't. I can check down at the general store for you if—"

"Don't worry about it." She sat back. "Definitely not worth that much trouble. Just had a cravin' is all."

Sliding his chair back, Garrett stood. "Do you want me—"

"No. Both of you. It's fine." She gestured to Garrett. "Sit down. It ain't that big a deal."

The two men looked at each other and seemed to come to an agreement not to push it. Garrett sat and the clerk nodded and walked back to his desk.

Returning to his meal, Garrett swirled a cube of steak in the pool of gravy on his plate. After a few moments of silence, he quietly hummed. He looked up at her and smiled as the beautiful melody escaped his lips. His small frame, boyish looks and honest demeanor made her feel slightly sorry for him. In a world full of brutes and killers, many of whom were twice his size, Garrett just didn't seem to fit. He was like a little brother who was way too eager to impress. She couldn't help but enjoy his company.

Abigail broke off a piece of cornbread. "Where you off to next?"

Garrett's humming stopped abruptly. His smile disappeared. "Well ... I hadn't really decided."

"Back to Helena?"

"Maybe." He swallowed another piece of steak. "Are *you* going back to Helena?"

"No."

"Oh." His voice dropped in volume. "Where to then?"

Abigail placed the piece of cornbread in her mouth. It was dry and flavorless and instantly parched her palate. "Was thinkin' I'd head to the train station in Logan." She swallowed and picked at her front teeth with her tongue. "Ride it back to Idaho."

Garrett lowered his fork. "What's in Idaho?"

"Just got some business to take care of."

"Never been to Logan. Think maybe they'd have some work for a driver there?"

"Possibly."

"Would you, um …"

"I'd love the company, yes."

Garrett's eyes lit up. His smile returned. "Alright! Sounds great." He chewed and swallowed the remains of his meal. "Didn't you say your father was in Idaho? You going back to take care of him?"

Abigail broke off another piece of the cornbread and crushed it between her thumb and forefinger. "My father was murdered …" She slowly sprinkled the crumbs around her plate. "… and I'm going to kill the man that did it."

TWENTY

"SHOULDN'T WE GO a little faster?" Nat said as they made their way down the eastern side of the rise.

"We go too fast, they'll know we saw 'em."

"But we *did* see them. Besides, a hoof print is a hoof print, right? How they going to know if it was fast or slow?"

"A galloping horse's prints are farther apart." Beckett looked over his shoulder. "They'll know."

"But why does it matter?"

"Because I want to find out who these guys are and I can't do that if they know we're on to them."

As they reached a small clearing, Beckett stopped his sorrel and slid from the saddle. "Help me build a fire."

"What?"

"Less questions. More doing." Beckett hurriedly collected sticks and twigs. "Quickly!"

"But I thought—"

"Just do it."

As soon as the fire was established Beckett climbed back onto his sorrel. "Let's go."

Nat followed without a word. Either he'd figured out what Beckett was up to or he'd just given up asking. After continuing east into the trees at a reasonable pace for a few dozen yards, Beckett abruptly turned south. "*Now* we hurry. But quietly."

"We're doubling back on them aren't we?"

Beckett smiled and kicked his sorrel to a gallop.

ROBARGE PACED ALONG the edge of the ridge, studying the ground which was made up of loose dirt over shale.

"They stopped here but didn't camp."

"Maybe one of 'em had to take a piss," Holton said.

"Or a shit." Quincey chuckled. "Hey, Drew. Why don't you hop down and check.

"Fuck off, Manny."

Robarge mounted his Appaloosa. "They're still heading east."

"Really?" Quincey said. "I ain't no expert tracker and I could've told you that. They're always 'still heading east'."

Turning his horse, Robarge sidled next to Quincey, pulled the sawed-off shotgun from the holster on his back and placed it under his chin. "If I want your input ..." He pulled back both hammers. "... I will ask for it."

Quincey trembled against the barrel. "Yes sir. Sorry sir."

Robarge looked him in the eye for five seconds then removed the gun from his chin. Lowering the hammers, he returned it to its holster and turned his horse. "Shall we?"

LOW PINE BOUGHS stung Beckett's face as they tore through the trees. They'd gone south for a quarter mile at full gallop before looping back to the west. Nat followed closely behind on his mare. Baxter hopped logs and dodged trees a few yards back.

Just before they reached the base of the rise they'd come down earlier, Beckett reined his sorrel to a stop and hopped off.

"I want you to stay here with the horses. Don't dismount." He removed his coat and threw it over his saddle horn. "Make sure the dog stays too. I'll check them out then come back. Just be ready."

Nat slid the revolver he'd taken off of the fat man at Frank's cabin from its holster. "You want to take this? You're not armed."

Beckett placed his hand on his Bowie. "I'll be fine. Besides, I just gonna see what they want. Don't plan on gettin' in a fight."

Chuckling, Nat slid the revolver back into the holster. "Yeah, we'll see."

ROBARGE STOPPED his Appaloosa the second he smelled smoke from a green fire wafting through the trees. He held his hand up, halting the men behind him then backed his horse to them.

"Dismount then tie off your horses. We'll go at them on foot."

Both Quincey and Holton nodded and complied. Once they were all on the ground and armed, Robarge leaned in close.

"I'll head straight in the way they came. Holton, you come at them from the north, Quincey, from the south. Stop a few yards from the tree line. Don't let them see you. I'll make the first move. Don't do anything until I give you a signal.

The two men nodded and headed off in different directions.

Before they got too far, Robarge breathily called after them. "And be quiet."

BECKETT CAME ACROSS the path they'd traveled on horseback earlier. There were three new sets of hoof prints in addition to their own. He crouched and followed where they led into trees. Above him, the cold wind had brought menacing dark clouds from the east. The air temperature dropped suddenly as he felt the first large drop hit his shoulder.

As the rain slowly increased, he came across three horses tied to trees just beyond the fire he and Nat had built. Next to a flea-bitten gray was an old mare and across from them was a beautiful Appaloosa.

"Perfect."

Beckett ran to the Appaloosa, unhitched and removed the saddle then threw it aside. After doing the same to the remaining horses, he untied them and slapped them on the rear in turn, sending them trotting away from the fire.

A LARGE RAINDROP hit the brim of Robarge's hat as he neared the tree line. Another hit him on the shoulder followed by one on the neck as he reached the fire. The clearing was only a few yards in diameter. The small fire sat in its center. That was it. No horses. No men.

"Shit."

He pulled the sawed-off from his back and reversed into the trees.

To his right he heard rustling and the hollow, muted sound of a body taking a blow. A low thud reverberated through the trees from where Quincey had been positioned.

"Valentine?" Robarge turned toward the sound. "I know it's you."

BECKETT SHOOK THE STING from his hand as he heard his name. The slow man with the single-barrel shotgun lay at his feet.

"We just want to talk." The voice echoed across the clearing and through the trees.

It came from the west where they'd ridden earlier. Beckett hurried around the eastern edge of the clearing, making sure to keep out of sight. The rain was coming down persistently now, the rhythmic pattering on the ground drowning out his footfalls.

Once he'd reached the northern section, he saw a small man with a rusty revolver crouched behind a bush, his attention focused on the fire. A few moments later Beckett was upon him. As the small man raised his gun, Beckett's elbow caught him on the temple, toppling him.

A SHARP CRACK followed by a low thud came from the north where Holton was stationed. Robarge pulled the hammers back on his shotgun and bolted toward the sound. Rain peppered his face as he skirted the clearing. A moment later he found Holton's body lying in the quickly-softening dirt.

He felt a presence behind him then cold steel on his throat.

BECKETT PRESSED his fourteen-inch Bowie against the short, dark man's skin.

"Drop it."

The man paused a beat then tossed his sawed-off shotgun aside.

"Who are you?" Beckett pulled the man in closer.

"I work for Mister Cain."

"Sheriff Cain is dead."

"I work for his son."

Beckett gently pulled his Bowie across the man's skin. A trickle of blood followed. The man didn't flinch.

"His son's are dead too."

"Not all of them."

ROBARGE COULD TELL the statement caught Valentine off guard. Slowly he reached for his cross-holstered double-action Colt. He could feel the cool impression of the inlayed skull on his right hand as he pulled the trigger in lightning-quick succession. Twisting against Valentine, he emptied the chamber through the end of his holster, hoping to catch him with at least one of the rounds.

BECKETT PUSHED the man aside and dove away as the gun went off. The last round tore through the fabric of his pants. Beckett reached down and felt the warmth of the pulsing wound on his thigh. Turning, he ran through the clearing and back to Nat and the horses, limping against the pain.

Behind him he heard the sound of the dark man's sawed-off shotgun exploding. The first shot landed somewhere to his left, the second breezed past him to his right, a few of the pellets catching him on the right flank. He fell against a tree for a moment then continued running.

When he reached Nat and the horses, he grabbed the reins of his sorrel and put his foot in the stirrup.

"What the hell is going on? I heard gunfire."

Beckett pulled himself onto his saddle, grunting from the pain. "Let's get out of here."

"Are you hit? You're bleeding."

Turning his horse southeast, Beckett kicked it to a gallop, plowing through heavy sheets of rain.

TWENTY-ONE

TEN MINUTES LATER they came across a large river, swelling and churning from the now massive downpour. Water engulfed the banks, uprooting small saplings and bushes, dragging them downstream. Distant flashes lit the eastern horizon followed by rolling waves of thunder. With each strike the interval between light and sound diminished.

Beckett slid his sorrel to a stop just before the waterline. Nat reined in his mare behind him followed by Baxter.

"Shit, Beckett. What are we going to do? We can't cross that."

Beckett removed his hat and stuffed it into his saddlebag. "We ain't got no choice."

"Cant't we go around?"

"That's the Bitterroot. It runs from Missoula to the next territory. There ain't no way around. With the rain coming down like this, there ain't gonna be a better time neither."

Just to the north, a twenty-foot alder slowly tipped then fell into the current. It raced past them taking down two smaller trees in its path.

"There ain't no better time? You've got to be kidding me."

"If we wait until it settles down, our friends back there will be on us. If we go across now, it'll be worse by the time they get here. They'll have no choice but to wait it out."

"They've got to be right behind us." Nat turned in his saddle.

"Nah. I took care of that."

Nat shook his head. "Of course you did."

"You should go first. I'll follow just in case something goes wrong."

"Oh, I'm sure something will go wrong." Nat jerked his bowler off of his head and slid it under one of his suspenders. "What about Baxter?"

Beckett looked down to see the mutt huddled and shivering beneath his horse. "I'll take the dog. You just get going. Keep tight to your mount and don't let go. She'll make it across with or without you."

"Thanks for the confidence."

As Nat eased his mare toward the rapids, Beckett hopped down from his sorrel and scooped up the soggy mutt. When he slid back into his saddle he held the dog next to him and across his lap. Another lightning bolt lit the trees around them like a photographer's flash powder, almost instantly followed by a gigantic explosion from above. He could feel Baxter trembling as he led his sorrel into the water.

Nat's mare seemed to have little problem fording the first two-thirds of the river. As they neared the far edge though, it was spooked by another crack of thunder and momentarily lost its balance, tipping Nat toward the rapids. As he clung to his saddle horn and righted himself, the mare froze in the raging water. Kicking and yelling, Nat eventually got it moving and out onto the other side.

As Beckett's sorrel entered the river, the water level seemed to rise suddenly. The strengthening currents pushed and pulled at his leg and lapped up over the top of his saddle.

Half way through, at the deepest point, a large gust of wind pelted him in the face with stinging, hard rain, making Baxter shift across his lap. Beckett grasped the mutt tighter, pulling it closer.

"Whoa, there, buddy."

Baxter's shivering vibrated through Beckett's chest.

"It'll be okay. We're almost—"

A giant explosion of light and sound ripped through him and lit the forest like midday. The lightning struck a tree just upstream sending the full upper half into the rapids. Splinters of wood rained down. The remaining trunk glowed, engulfed in flames.

Beckett's sorrel reared at the sound and turned downstream, throwing him off balance. As he worked to right himself, Baxter slid from his lap and into the rapids. The current quickly pulled the dog under.

ROBARGE SLID his freshly-loaded shotgun into its holster and worked at emptying and reloading his Colt as he ran through the trees.

"Holton. Quincey. Get the hell up!"

As he wiped a diluted stream of blood from the cut below his Adam's apple, he found his saddle lying upside-down in the mud where his Appaloosa should have been.

"Son of a bitch."

Quincey came stumbling out of the trees behind him, grasping his chest. "The horses. They're runnin' loose. Saw yours on the way here."

"Where?"

Quincey grunted and pointed to the south. "Over there."

Robarge took off running past him. The rain was coming down harder now. He could hear thunder rolling in the distance.

He found his horse grazing beneath a pine. Robarge grabbed the reins, pulled it toward a log and used it to hop on, bareback. He turned the reins in his left hand, unholstered his shotgun with his right and kicked his Appaloosa to a gallop.

THE CACOPHONY of the storm ceased as Beckett's head disappeared beneath the rapids. Water rushed into his nose and mouth and worked to pull him farther under. Using all of his strength, he kicked and thrashed until he could breathe again.

He saw his sorrel a few yards upstream, making its way out of the water. Nat grabbed the reins and yelled something in his direction. Beckett turned and looked downstream for the mutt. Whitecaps lapped over his head and around him. One of them almost pulled him under again.

As he eased himself to the eastern shoreline, he saw a small black nose emerging from the froth. A moment later, Baxter's head popped out of the water, the dog's forelegs frantically clawing toward him only a few feet away. Beckett dove in the mutt's direction and let the current pull him along.

He grabbed Baxter by the neck scruff, pulling the mutt close as they continued down stream. They quickly came upon a downed tree jutting out into the river. Beckett grasped it with his free hand and held tight. The sudden stop of momentum pulled them beneath the rapids. He clawed his way along the thin trunk until his head cleared the water again. A few moments later they were on the eastern bank.

Beckett rolled onto his back and caught his breath. The thick downpour filled his mouth and nose. Turning over, he saw Baxter lying in the mud next to him, paws outstretched, head facing away. As Beckett reached out to the dog, it turned toward him, tongue flapping, stump wagging. Baxter eased next to him and frantically licked his face.

"I can't believe what I just saw." Nat slid from his mare and knelt next to them, holding his hand out. "I thought you were a goner."

Beckett took the hand and let his partner help pull him up. "Not quite yet."

Nat fell back to his knees and embraced the dog. Baxter licked him as well. "I thought you were *both* dead."

Beckett leaned against his sorrel that Nat had tied to his saddle horn. "So did I."

As Beckett looked down at Nat and Baxter, the ground at his feet exploded, sending shards of river rock against his shins. He looked across the river to see a figure standing next to an unsaddled Appaloosa.

"Look out!" Beckett yelled, pulling his sorrel into the trees.

Nat stood and ran to his mare. As the second blast hit a tree to their left, he pulled the ten-gauge from his saddle.

"Nat, wait."

Pointing the large shotgun toward the figure on the western bank, Nat pulled the first trigger. The huge blast made him stagger. As soon as he caught his balance from the recoil, he pulled the second trigger.

Beckett couldn't tell for sure but he thought he saw the figure across the river fall to the ground.

"Get on your horse and let's get out of here."

Nat slid the shotgun back into his saddle holster and hopped on. "I'm right with you."

TWENTY-TWO

THE RIDE FROM RADERSBURGH to Logan had been uneventful. After staying in separate rooms at the Patterson Hotel, they'd hit the trail at sunup and did not stop. Garrett was glad that Abigail again had chosen to bounce along next to him on the bench of his wagon instead of riding her palomino mare but was upset with himself for being too afraid to say two words to her the entire day-long trip. He'd opened his mouth more than a dozen times to comment on how the mountains looked in the sunlight or how the flowers around them smelled, but he could never follow through.

The young woman sitting next to him was a true mystery. On the outside, Abigail was strong, forthright and highly intimidating—especially to a man like himself. But on the inside, behind her delicate green eyes was something hidden. Something softer.

She was patient with and very kind to Garrett—more so than she'd been to any other person they'd encountered—but she was still extremely distant and guarded. The only hint at softness he'd seen was the special care she'd taken when interacting with her beautiful palomino. Abigail would stroke its mane and whisper to it as she rode or moved it from here to there. She treated the animal as if it was her only true friend. As if it was the only creature in the world she could trust.

Garrett was keenly aware of this as she casually untied the mare from his wagon outside of Logan's train depot. She quietly clicked her tongue in the mare's ear and ran her fingers through its coarse blonde mane as she walked it the few steps to a hitch outside. After looping her reins around the post, she brushed the road dust from her dress and looked up at Garrett who was still perched on his bench.

"Well, I guess this is it." There was a definite finality in her tone.

He found it hard to look in her direction. "Yes, Miss Abigail, I guess it is."

"I'm sure you'll find work here in town. Always someone in need of a lift."

"Always someone," he reluctantly agreed.

"Oh, I almost forgot." She took a couple of steps up to his side of the wagon.

Garrett looked down at her. A pang of hope shot through him.

Abigail stretched her hand out. "My bag."

He looked down at the long leather pack at his feet that carried her Henry rifle. The hope dwindled as he picked it up and leaned over to hand it to her. Abigail lifted up on her toes and gave him a brief, delicate kiss on the cheek. It caught him so off guard that he almost fell from his bench.

"Take care of yourself, Garrett. I mean it." She ran her soft thumb along the stubble of his jaw then stepped back.

Garrett sat in a stupor for a few seconds. He realized his mouth was hanging open when he saw her chuckle. "I-I will." He tried to compose himself. "You too."

She tied the leather pack to her saddle and gave him one last smile. "I always do."

Then Abigail disappeared into the train depot.

***

GARRETT DROVE his wagon, slowly and hopelessly across Logan and finally stopped outside of the last saloon in town. He was no friend to alcohol but he'd decided that the regret and a headache a night of drinking would bring would help take his mind off of the woman he'd just left. Tying his horses to the hitch, he wandered toward the chatter and buzz that emanated from the doorway of the bar. As he placed his hand onto the peeling paint of a batwing, an idea came to him.

He took a couple of steps back across the sidewalk then jumped down to the street. After scanning the buildings on both sides, he found the one he was looking for and bolted toward it. Garrett was in such a hurry he almost knocked over an old man loading a cart of chickens. Apologizing profusely, he helped the man right himself then continued up and into Hawthorne's General Store.

As Garrett slid into the center of the room, the proprietor popped up from behind the counter.

"Howdy, mister. Somethin' I can help you find?"

A THOUSAND YESTERDAYS

Three minutes later Garrett was running down the street at a full clip. Logan's main road spanned about a mile from the saloon where he'd left his wagon to the train depot at the far end. As he neared the depot, his lungs burned and he could feel bile rise from his stomach to the back of his throat. He hopped up onto the loading platform behind the depot and coughed up a mass of phlegm that he quickly spat behind a barrel.

When he collected himself, he glanced around the platform to find it completely empty of passengers. Walking to the edge, he looked up and down the track. There was no sign of a train. Had it already come and gone? He couldn't recall hearing a locomotive on his trip to the saloon but he'd been in such a foul mood that he easily could have missed it. Feeling the weight of the situation on his shoulders, he slumped onto a bench and let out a deep, pained sigh.

***

THE SUN WAS LOW and red when Garrett again pushed open the batwings of the saloon at the far end of town. The long return trip from the empty train depot seemed to take a lifetime. As he sat at the bar, the bartender placed an empty glass in front of him.

"What'll it be? Look like you need something strong."

"Whatever everyone else is drinking I guess."

The bartender spun, grabbed a tall bottle from behind the bar, turned and filled the glass. Amber liquid splashed over the edge forming a puddle on the wood. As Garrett lifted the glass, the commotion of the room behind him lulled. A moment later he felt a presence over his shoulder.

"Thought you wasn't much of a drinker."

Garrett turned to see Abigail slide up the bar and take the seat next to him. In his shock he dropped the glass of alcohol onto the dusty floor.

She smiled and turned toward the bartender. "Looks like my friend here's gonna need another. Actually, why don't you make that two?"

TWENTY-THREE

"BECKETT, WE'VE GOT TO STOP and rest," Nat yelled from his tired and panting mare. "We keep going like this we're going to kill the horses."

Nat heard no response. His partner just continued through the pines up ahead.

Reining in his mare, Nat hopped from his saddle and took a deep breath. "For the love of god, *stop*! They're not going to catch us."

As if hearing him for the first time, Beckett slowed his sorrel to a halt, paused for a beat then turned in his saddle.

"We rode hard through the night and we've been riding even harder all day. There's no way they can be close." Nat threw aside his reins, leaned against a tree and slid to the ground. "We need to rest."

As soon as he hit the dirt, Baxter came bounding through the trees and collapsed next to him, tongue flapping.

"Besides, I'm afraid you're going to bleed to death."

Beckett looked down at his blood-soaked pant leg then ran his hand under his coat along his wounded flank. "It ain't that bad." He took a deep breath and winced. "I've had worse."

"I'm sure you have. Probably deserved it too."

Turning his sorrel, Beckett eased his way toward Nat and slid from the saddle. He took a few steps in the direction they'd come and peered into the endless expanse of pine trees.

"With you dismantling their horses and that flooded river, they've got to be a day behind." Nat removed his coat and closed his eyes. A thin ray of late afternoon sunshine broke through the trees and bathed his face.

"At least a day," Beckett conceded after a long moment.

"Then get that pack of yours and patch yourself up." Nat lifted himself off the ground. "I'm going to start a fire."

Beckett turned to disagree but Nat cut him off.

"I'll make one of your damn tiny Indian ones. Don't worry."

* * *

AFTER UNSADDLING the horses and leading them to a nearby stream, Beckett returned to the small fire Nat had built. It was big enough to give off heat but inconspicuous enough not to be noticed. Just like he would have made. He was impressed.

Beckett pulled a small pouch from his saddle and a roll of bandages from his teardrop-shaped bag and sat on the cold, hard earth. Using his index fingers, he carefully ripped open the bloody hole in his pant leg. After doing the same to the long underwear beneath, he examined the wound. The bullet seemed to have only grazed the flesh.

Across the fire Nat took a swig from one of his bottles of gin.

Holding out his hand, Beckett gestured to it. "You mind?"

"Not at all." Nat stood and passed it over. "I've got some whiskey too if you'd prefer—"

Beckett took the bottle and poured a generous amount over his wound. The crusted and congealed blood slowly disappeared revealing a long, ragged gash. It wasn't deep and had already begun to heal.

"Jesus, Beckett. Not my gin."

Beckett peeled a bandage from the roll and wrapped it around his leg. He then opened the small pouch, retrieving a needle and some black thread. After stitched up his pants, he removed his coat and shirt and pulled off the upper half of his long underwear. He carefully touched the half-dozen puncture wounds peppered across his right flank.

"Think I might need your help here."

Nat stood, pulled a bottle of whiskey from his saddlebag then walked around to Beckett's side of the fire. "Here." He handed the bottle over. "I'm not wasting any more of my gin on your worthless hide."

Beckett popped the cork with his teeth and carefully poured half the bottle across his flank, flinching with the effort. "There's some tweezers in that pouch. I need you to remove the pellets from my side. They ain't too deep."

Kneeling down, Nat found the rusty tweezers and examined the wounds.

"Douse 'em with whiskey." Beckett handed over the bottle.

Nat turned the tweezers beneath a steady stream of the amber liquid, handed back the bottle and sat at the ready.

"Alright." Beckett took a long swig. "Start diggin'."

Without hesitation, Nat attacked the first wound. Beckett recoiled from the pain then steadied himself.

"So, what did you learn?" Nat dropped the first pellet into the dirt and went after another.

Beckett flinched again. "What do you mean?"

"From our friends back there. Did you find out what they are after us for? You know, other than the obvious." He dropped the second pellet.

"Two of them are nothing." Beckett grit his teeth as the tweezers bore into the third hole. "Just a couple of the sheriff's useless thugs. Both looked familiar."

Nat found the lead pellet and pulled it out. He quickly went in for another.

"Whoa, hold on a sec." Beckett held up his hand. He took a couple of deep breaths and a long pull from the whiskey bottle. "Alright. Go ahead—"

Nat dug in for a fourth time. "And what about the leader? The mean one with the sawed-off."

Beckett exhaled as the tweezers exited his side. "He's someone new. Said he works for Cain's son. One we didn't kill."

"Zebediah." Nat dropped the lead ball and continued digging. "Heard Harvey and Doc talking about him. Was supposed to take over the sheriff's operations in Temperance. He's that big-shot gunfighter I was telling you about." The fifth pellet hit the dirt.

Panting, Beckett waved Nat off. "Jesus. How many we got left?"

"Just the one." Nat probed again.

Beckett almost fell over. "Shit!" He propped himself up. "Zebediah Cain?"

"You know him?" Nat dug in deeper. "Damn. This one's way in there."

Slumping over, Beckett caught his breath. "No." He grunted and ground his teeth. "Name's familiar though. Like I knew it in another life."

Beckett yelled as Nat ripped out the last pellet.

"Ha! Got you you little bastard." Nat threw the lead ball aside. "All clear."

Falling into the dirt, Beckett panted for a moment. "Take that bottle and—"

Nat poured the remains of the whiskey across Beckett's fresh wounds.

"Goddamn!"

Nat dropped the bottle in the dirt. "Feel better?"

Beckett smiled, his face against the cold earth. "Much."

"You're welcome." After putting the tweezers back into the small pouch Nat returned to his side of the fire. "Should we get back on the road?" He took a long swig from his bottle of gin.

Beckett didn't move. The damp ground felt good against his face. "Very funny."

"I don't know." Nat took another swig and kicked off his shoes. "If we don't hurry they might catch up to us."

"We're only a couple of days out of Silver Bow. There's … no … way …"

Beckett passed out before he could finish.

TWENTY-FOUR

ABIGAIL WAS WELL AWARE her presence had quieted the room. She'd found that not many women frequented saloons in the West. Some thought it taboo and against God's will. Others just did not want to be seen around whores. None of this bothered Abigail, though. She liked to have an occasional drink and she liked to have it around others. Even if they were mostly dirty, loud-mouth cowboys and miners with wandering eyes. Honestly, she didn't mind the attention.

This saloon was different from most. It was wide but not very deep with a very high ceiling. It did not appear to house any whores. Instead there seemed to be some sort of storage or possibly a shipping depot behind the back wall. Along the front wall below curtained windows were three booths with tables and back-to-back benches. All were filled with men eating plates of food, implying the back room must house a kitchen as well. Metal utensils clinked on plates breaking the silence.

Abigail sat next to Garrett at a small bar to the left of the weathered batwings with their backs to the rest of the saloon. A large mirror behind the bar gave her a view of the whole room. Five tables filled the area, all of which were occupied by groups of card players. One table in particular had been very boisterous when she'd walked in. Now, its three occupants, cowboys who looked to be fresh off the range, sat in silence as she caught them eyeing her in the mirror's reflection.

The bartender set two glasses down and filled them with whiskey. He slid one to her and the other to Garrett who sat staring at her in shock, his mouth hanging open as usual.

Abigail picked up her glass and downed half of it. It wasn't very good.

After a nearly a minute Garrett finally squeaked out a few words. "Thought you were on the train."

"There ain't no train." Abigail drank the rest of her glass. "Don't come through 'til tomorrow, I guess."

Garrett seemed to be trying to comprehend the answer. "Not until tomorrow?"

"Nope. Runs every other day."

A subtle smile crossed Garrett's face. He quickly concealed it by rubbing his jaw.

"Every other day?"

Abigail raised her eyebrows and chuckled. "Yes, Garrett. It's true. I'll be here until tomorrow. Repeating everything I say aint' gonna make it *more* true."

"I didn't mean to ... I'm just—"

"I know what you meant. I'm glad to see you, too."

Garrett slumped on his stool as if he were melting in the sun. He placed his hands on the bar to steady himself, obvious elation in his eyes.

Abigail turned away and swirled the few remaining drops of whiskey in her glass.

"Another, miss?" The bartender held up the bottle.

She nodded and pushed the glass toward him.

The volume of the room slowly grew as the novelty of her presence wore off. The three loud-mouthed cowboys had resumed their game. One of them called for another round.

After filling Abigail's glass, the bartender grabbed a couple of bottles from under the bar and went to service his other customers.

She could feel Garrett's eyes on her. "You—" He cleared his throat and lowered his voice. "You still going after the fella who shot your pa?"

Abigail traced the rim of the glass with her finger. She stopped when it reached a large chip on the far side. "Yes."

"You sure that's the right thing to do?"

"Don't really give a shit if it's right or wrong. It needs to be done."

Garrett turned away. She could feel him tense up.

Abigail ran her finger around the smooth rim slowly in the opposite direction. "And I'm the one who's got to do it."

"Why not the sheriff?" Garrett was almost pleading. "That's what lawmen are for. They go after bad men."

She pressed harder on the glass. The added friction caused her finger to jerk along the rim in an irregular rhythm that reminded her of a telegraph operator tapping out a message. "He's a deputy. He *works* for the sheriff. Calls himself Cincinnati. He killed my father and shot me. Then he let his men—" Her fingertip hit the chip in the rim of the glass. She could feel it pierce the calloused skin. "They all need to die."

"But why do you have to do it alone? There's got to be someone who can help."

Abigail lifted her finger from the glass and looked at it. Blood beaded from the edge of the thin cut. Soon the whole wound was red. "A friend of my father's came to stay with us for a couple of days ..." The drop moved along the edge of her finger. "... before this all happened. I liked him. I liked him more than any man I'd ever met. He was strong and confident and wasn't afraid of the sheriff or his deputies. He stood to them and their guns with only a knife." The drop flowed evenly until it hit the crease behind her first knuckle where it stopped and pooled. "He was crazy. He had to be. Said he'd take care of our problem. Said he'd go after the sheriff and his men ... with just his knife." The pool escaped the crease behind her knuckle "I'm worried Cincinnati killed him too." She placed her finger in her mouth and tasted the fresh blood.

"You ain't no killer, Abigail. I just know it."

She removed the finger from her mouth and examined it. The bleeding had stopped. "Tell that to those three road agents we left up on that ridge."

Garrett shook his head. "That was self-defense. What you're talking about is cold-blooded vengeance. It's completely different."

"Is it?"

"Those men on the ridge had their guns on us. Hell, that one had his gun in my mouth. By shootin' them you saved our lives." Garrett swallowed with an audible gulp. "Killin' this fella for what he did to your pa and maybe your friend ... it's pure vigilantism. It'll be murder, Abigail. Are you sure you want that weight on your shoulders—that price on your head?"

"Well, Mister Garrett ..." She grabbed her glass of whiskey and downed it. "... I guess I'm just gonna have to find that out."

After a moment of contemplation, Garrett followed her lead and downed his own whiskey. He slapped the glass back onto the bar then let out a deep, breathy cough. His eyes watered as he convulsed on the stool next to her.

Reaching over, Abigail patted him on the back. "You alright?"

Garrett waved her off then croaked out, "I want to go with you."

"What?"

"I want to go with you. To Idaho."

"Garrett, you can't—"

"I can help." He coughed again. "I need to help. I won't let you go alone."

"These men ... they're pure evil. I don't want you to get hurt."

Garrett straightened up and turned toward her. He wiped his eyes and met hers. "I'm going with you." He slapped the bar with his left hand. "I won't take 'no' for an answer."

She could tell he was trying to be firm but as soon as he said it, his eyes pleaded for her approval. After staring into them, she knew he wouldn't give up.

Abigail smiled. "Fine. I guess I could use the help."

"That's great! I—"

"But only if you do exactly what I say when I say it."

Garrett nodded "Deal."

"If I think it's too dangerous and I tell you to run, you run"

"Got it."

Abigail looked into his eyes again. Garrett's usual eager expression had returned. A smile crossed his boyish face.

"You're crazy. You do know that don't you?"

"Sure do, Miss Abigail. I sure do."

Shaking her head, she scanned the room through the mirror for the bartender. "I think we *both* need another drink."

One of the booths by the door cleared out as the bartender collected some coins from the table. He met Abigail's eyes, nodded and turned back toward the bar. The table of three cowboys was as rowdy as ever. They had ceased playing cards and had moved on to showing off their gun-spinning skills ... or in this case, lack there of. Abigail rolled her eyes.

"Oh, I almost forgot." Garrett slid his hand into his coat pocket. "I got something for you at the store earlier …"

As Garrett pulled a small brown bag from his pocket, Abigail caught one of the cowboys awkwardly spinning his

Colt revolver in the mirror's reflection. He pushed his chair back and stood.

"Would you look at that, boys?" The gun wobbled on his finger as it flipped end-over-end. His companions laughed and cheered him on. "I'm like a regular ol' Wyatt —"

The gun slid from his finger, landed upside-down against the tabletop and went off.

Abigail flinched from the sound and watched the cowboy's image disappear as the mirror behind the bar shattered. Shards of glass crumbled from the wall and rained across the floor.

"Jesus Christ!" The bartender dropped an open bottle onto the bar as he dove for cover.

Whiskey splashed and sprinkled across Abigail's face, momentarily blinding her. She rubbed the sting from her eyes and looked at her hands through blurred vision. As the image cleared, she realized that she'd not only wiped whiskey from her face but also blood. Her hands were covered in the sticky dark liquid.

Panic rose as she searched her body for pain.

Had she been shot?

The question was answered when she saw Garrett's head drop to the bar. His stool slid backwards as his body slumped forward.

"Garrett?"

He was facing her with his cheek against the bar. Blood bubbled from a large, mangled exit wound below his chin and poured onto the floor.

"Garrett!" Abigail slid over to him and cradled his face with her hands. "No, no, *no!*"

She looked into his open eyes. There was nothing behind them.

As she held his face, his limp body toppled from his stool and he slid to the floor. She followed Garrett to the ground and leaned over him.

"No. Don't let this happen. Please."

As she ran her bloody hand through his hair, she realized Garrett's arm was resting against her thigh. In it was the paper bag he'd removed from his coat. She carefully slid it from his fingers and let the contents drop into her open hand.

Garrett had bought her two bars of wax-paper wrapped chocolate. She held them to her chest. A tear ran down her cheek as she touched Garrett's face.

"Jesus, Dwight. I think you scared that feller to death." One of the cowboys behind her laughed.

"Yup. Scared him right out of his seat," said another cowboy.

"Guess I better keep practicing." The cowboy who dropped the gun laughed and holstered his revolver. "You know miss, you might want to get yourself a boyfriend who ain't so yeller."

Abigail felt the anger build up inside her. Adrenaline pumped in her ears and her eyes burned. She stood and slid Garrett's present into the pocket of her skirt.

She turned toward the three cowboys. Her hands hovered over her pearl-handled Colts.

"Draw."

A THOUSAND YESTERDAYS

The three cowboys looked at each other then back at her.

"I said draw!"

TWENTY-FIVE

"**WHOA THERE, MISS.**" The cowboy at the right of the table moved his hands in a "slow down" motion. "Dwight didn't mean nothin' by it. Was just an accident."

"Yeah. He didn't mean nothin'," agreed the cowboy in the middle.

Abigail stared the three men down. After she'd told them to draw, the two who'd been seated slowly stood to confront her.

The cowboy on the left whose gun had killed Garrett—the one they called Dwight—was greasy, short and nervous.

The tallest of the group stood in the middle with his back to the wall. He was well over six feet and had long blonde hair that escaped from beneath a tattered hat. At his side was an old black-powder revolver.

To the right was the most dangerous looking of the three. A blued-steel Colt hung low against his right thigh and a Bowie was sheathed on his left. It was a large knife but not the biggest she'd seen. His hands were frozen in their "slow down" pose.

"Your friend shouldn't have been sitting there." Dwight's tone was accusing.

"Hey now, Dwight. It wasn't the kid's fault," the man with the Bowie said. "I think if we all just—"

"Draw your gun now, you goddamn coward." Abigail took a step toward Dwight.

He took a quick step back and almost fell over his chair. "You better not be threatening me."

"And what if I am?" She took another step closer. "Why don't you do something about it, you son of a bitch?"

"I know you ain't havin' the best night but, miss, you really got to calm down." The man with the Bowie slowly lowered his hands to his sides. "We don't want no trouble."

"I ain't gonna let no bitch talk to me like that." Dwight lowered his hand to his Colt. "If she want's trouble, I'll give it to her."

"Then give it to me." Abigail stepped toward him again. "I know your tiny pecker won't."

Dwight's eyes widened. A flush of red filled his cheeks.

The man with the Bowie placed his palm on his polished revolver. "Dwight, don't—"

Dwight grabbed his gun.

Abigail's right-hand Colt was out before he could clear his holster. Her first two shots tore through Dwight's shoulder. She took another step closer and put a bullet through his Adam's apple.

The man with the Bowie cleared his gun and pointed it. He was about to squeeze the trigger when Abigail drew her left-hand Colt and put two bullets in his chest. As he twisted and fell to his right, his gun went off, hitting the middle cowboy in the knee.

Blood and bone exploded from the tall cowboy's leg. As soon as he touched his black-powder revolver, Abigail put a bullet from each gun into his skull. Falling backwards agains the wall, his body toppled to the left and landed hard on the floor.

Abigail stepped through the haze of black smoke to their table and shoved it aside with her hip. She stood over the man with the Bowie as he struggled to raise his gun. Her right-hand Colt echoed in the high-ceilinged room as she blew out the back of his head.

Finally she turned to the man who'd killed Garrett. He lay on the dusty floor of the saloon clenching his throat with both hands. Dark blood pulsed through his fingers and bubbled from his mouth. She watched him for a moment as he squirmed and struggled on the floor. His terrified eyes pleaded for death.

Abigail raised her left-hand Colt and obliged him.

"Alright. That's enough," a voice from the batwings called. "I'm gonna need you to drop them guns, miss."

She slowly turned her head toward the doorway to see a man with a sheriff's badge filling the entrance. He leveled a Winchester at her.

"Please, miss. We don't need no more bloodshed here tonight."

Abigail looked down at the carnage she'd created. Three bodies lay around her. Blood pooled at her feet.

"Drop 'em," the sheriff said. "I ain't gonna tell you again."

Abigail waited a beat then carefully holstered her Colts and unbuckled her gun belt. She held it at arm's length as she stepped toward Garrett's body. After placing her guns on the bar, she knelt at his side.

"I'm sorry, Garrett." She placed the palm of her hand over his forehead and closed his eyelids then looked up at the sheriff. "I need to bury him."

"We'll get to that. First I need you to come with me."

"I ain't gonna leave him."

The sheriff sighed and softened his voice. "I promise you he'll be taken care of."

Abigail ran her fingers through Garrett's hair.

"But right now, miss … you and me need to have a little talk."

TWENTY-SIX

ZEBEDIAH SLOWLY pulled back the hammer.

Click. Click. CLICK. CLICK.

It had been years since he'd handled a Colt Single Action Army. He'd forgotten that the first two tones created by the precisely machined action were quieter than the second two. He slowly squeezed the trigger and carefully let the hammer down.

Holding the cylinder closer to his ear, he thumbed the hammer back again.

Click. Click. CLICK. CLICK.

Zebediah had watched Cincinnati do the exact thing many times over the years they spent doing bounty work together. His friend would place the cylinder of his polished-nickel peacemaker to his ear and work the hammer back, listening to the action.

"Do you hear that?" Cincinnati would say. "It spells C-O-L-T when you cock it."

Fingering the trigger, Zebediah again lowered the hammer. He turned Cincinnati's Colt in the soft evening light and watched as the amber sunset danced across its shiny surface like fire. His friend had taken immaculate care of the gun over the years—its mechanism was oiled and tuned, its finish polished—yet it had obviously been well used.

The hammer, trigger and trigger guard were worn down to the steel and small pock-marks traversed the barrel and cylinder, interrupting the smooth luster of the nickel finish. The ivory grips were well-worn and comfortable but had yellowed from years of contact with human skin. An angel-hair crack splintered the left grip halfway up from the heel and had been repaired with a dark brown putty or clay.

Zebediah placed the cylinder back to his ear and thumbed the hammer.

Click. Click. CLICK. CLICK.

"Goddamn you, Cincinnati." His voice was low and to himself. None of the train's passengers had chosen to sit near him. "How could you let that asshole kill you?"

The train's conductor passed Zebediah as he made his way through the aisle. He braced himself against one of the seat backs when the car lurched as the brakes took hold.

"Next stop, Ironwood." Regaining his balance, the conductor continued down the aisle. "This is the end of the line for the night, folks. Make sure to collect all of your belongings."

Zebediah leveled the Colt at the back of the conductor's head. He trailed the uniformed man's movements with the front sight as he neared the train car's front door.

"How could you let him kill you?" Zebediah said again.

The train conductor slid open the heavy door, stepped through and closed it behind him.

After a beat, Zebediah let the hammer down and lowered Cincinnati's gun. As he sat up and turned to his left, he saw an old woman staring at him in horror. She held a bag tight to her chest as if to protect herself from the evil she'd just witnessed.

"Just practicing my aim, ma'am. No need to get upset." Zebediah stood as the train jolted forward for the last time. He slid Cincinnati's gun behind his back and into his belt. "Could've been pointing it at you."

***

THREE MEN WERE WAITING for Zebediah when he exited the train. Recognizing two of them, he assumed the third was the man his father had appointed as head of the mining operation. Zebediah met them in the middle of the long railway platform.

The Korrigan brothers were almost as tall as Mordecai had been. Being identical twins, their faces shared the same hawk-like nose and sharp features. Thaddeus Korrigan wore a thin mustache that joined close-cropped sideburns at his jaw, the left of which was interrupted by a ragged scar that crossed his cheek. He wore chaps, spurs and a long duster. On his hips were matching Scofield model Smith & Wessons.

Reuben had on a similar set of clothes but instead of a duster he wore a short, rawhide coat with multiple pockets. He was clean-shaven and better looking than his brother. A '66 Winchester was propped against his shoulder and an ivory-handled Colt, very similar to Cincinnati's, was tied to his right leg.

The man between them wasn't short but wasn't as tall as the Korrigans or even Zebediah. His face was puffy and ruddy. A furry mustache hid his upper lip. He wore a tattered olive-tweed suit and no sidearm.

"Mr. Cain." The man held out his right hand. "I am Gilbert Higgins. I run your father's operation here."

Zebediah looked down at Higgins' hand but did not take it. Instead he turned to the Korrigans. "Good to see you boys. Thad. Reuben." He took each brother's hand and shook them in turn. "How you two holding up?"

"We're good Zeb," Thaddeus said.

"Sorry to hear 'bout Walter and your brothers." Reuben placed his hand on Zebediah's shoulder. "We'll get the asshole who done it."

Gilbert Higgins cleared his throat. "The wire you sent came through a couple of days ago. We've been preparing for your arrival."

Zebediah turned to the ruddy man, annoyed with his presence.

"One of our miners and his family have offered to put you up in a spare—"

"Where is your house?" Zebediah's tone was abrupt.

"Um, my wife and myself live on the north side of town. Just outside—"

"Good." Zebediah tried to picture the town in his head. "That should be fine. I'll need you out within the hour."

"Out of where? My house?" Higgins took a step back.

Zebediah turned back to the Korrigan brothers. "Is his wife a looker? She worth keeping around?"

Thaddeus scrunched up his face. Reuben simply shook his head.

"Make sure you take your woman with you." Zebediah pushed past Higgins and walked toward the train's livestock car. "I don't care where you go."

"Mr. Cain. This is highly irregular. You can't just kick my family out of our home."

"Give him a *half* hour," Zebediah said over his should to the brothers. "If he doesn't get his shit out of *my* house … shoot him."

TWENTY-SEVEN

PUSHING OPEN THE DOOR to the jail building, the sheriff gestured inside. "Have a seat." He stood back from the threshold to let Abigail pass.

The jail was not unlike others she'd seen. Two iron-barred cells sat against the far wall, their doors open. Each had a low cot and a ceramic wash basin. To the left were two wooden chairs and a small table. To the right was the sheriff's desk, behind which was a rack of rifles and shotguns. Wanted posters covered the room like patchwork wallpaper.

Abigail stepped through the office and into one of the cells.

"No. Miss …" The sheriff pointed to the two chairs across from his desk. "Have a seat."

Turning to face him, Abigail watched as he propped his Winchester in the corner, placed her gun belt on his desk and sat behind it.

She eyed him with curiosity.

"Please." The sheriff gestured to the chairs again.

After a long moment Abigail took the seat closest to the door.

The sheriff laced his hands behind his head and leaned his chair back. The rear legs creaked under his weight. He looked to be in his late fifties. The lines below his eyes and around his mouth showed years of stress. A thick gray ring of hair surrounded his glistening, sunburned head. He had a large frame but was surprisingly thin despite his protruding belly.

"Name's Pat Murphy. I'm Logan's sheriff, if you hadn't already guessed." He rocked his chair back an inch farther. "Who might you be?"

"Abigail Gibson."

"You related to ol' Deadeye Gibson outa Contention City?"

She sat up straight, looking out the open front door. "Not that I know of."

"Hmm." Sheriff Murphy tipped forward, the front legs of his chair booming against the floor. "I don't know quite what to make of you, Miss Gibson. Tell you the truth, I ain't never seen nothin' like what I saw back there ... and I've been in this business for a very long time. You familiar with those men you shot?"

"No."

"They work for a rancher outside of Bozeman. Come through here a few times a month. Do quite a lot of business with this town." Sheriff Murphy stood and walked around to the front of his desk. He crossed his arms over his belly and leaned against it. "And they were a real pain in my ass."

Abigail looked up and met the sheriff's eyes.

"Way I look at it, you did me a big favor back there. I saw everything. Saw them all pull first. Saw you put them all down. Would've—probably should've—stepped in but for some reason I knew you had it under control."

"They killed ..." Tears welled again but she choked them down. "... my friend."

"Saw that, too. In the eyes of the law you were justified. You were in the right. Swift justice. No trial. No fuss." He uncrossed his arms, placed his hands on the desktop and leaned back. "Just the way I like it."

Abigail looked through the door at the street. "If I ain't done nothing wrong, why take my guns and bring me here."

He stuck out his chin and scratched the stubble beneath it. "More for show than anything, really. Technically, vigilantes are still frowned upon 'round here."

"I ain't no vigilante. Just did what needed to be done."

"I don't disagree. Still ..." He shot his open left hand toward the door, gesturing at the town. "... people do talk. I doubt anyone in Logan would fault your actions but if I didn't bring you in ... well, it just wouldn't be proper."

"I don't give a shit if it's proper or not. I need to tend to Garrett's remains."

"I know and as I said, it will be taken care of." He placed his open hand agains his heart. "It would be my pleasure to do whatever is needed to put that poor friend of yours to rest. As soon as we're done here I'll go straight to the undertaker myself."

"As soon as we're *done* here? I thought you said I ain't done nothing wrong."

"You haven't. It's just ..." He ran his hand around his thick ring of gray hair and sighed. "... I want to offer you a job."

"A *what?*"

"Listen. I'm all alone here—as a lawman I mean. I could really use the help of someone with your talents. It's enough just keeping the peace in *town* let alone keeping up with all the warrants that come through—"

"I can't believe I'm hearing this." Abigail shot out of her chair and grabbed her gun belt.

"You'd have a chance to do what you did back there to other men who deserve it."

"Didn't kill them boys because I liked it. I did it because they murdered my friend." Buckling her belt, Abigail turned toward the door.

Sheriff Murphy stepped in front of her and placed his hands on her shoulders. "I get it. I really do. It's just ... you could be a big help. The bounties you'd be going after are for really bad men. Real killers. Real gunfighters."

"I ain't lookin' to be no bounty hunter." She glanced down at her holstered Colts and lowered her tone. "I got my own score to settle."

The sheriff let go of her shoulders, stepped back and studied her. "You're after somebody else." It was a statement not a question. There was genuine intrigue in his voice. "Is he around here? Let me help you. It's the least I could do."

Abigail sighed and looked up at him. "He ain't around here." She looked back out the door for a long moment. "He's back in Idaho."

"Idaho?" Hurrying behind his desk, Sheriff Murphy rifled through a stack of papers. "He wouldn't happen to be some big-shot gunfighter would he?"

Abigail furrowed her brow, cocked her head and looked at the sheriff.

When he found what he was searching for, he slammed it onto his desk. "Brown hair, even features, over six feet? Has a brand in the shape of a heart on his right forearm?"

Abigail thought of Cincinnati. His right forearm had been covered by a leather armband. She took a step toward the desk.

"Duke Valentine." Sheriff Murphy slid a freshly typed piece of paper across to her. "Wire came through from North Idaho with the warrant a couple of days ago. The huge reward caught my eye. Recall the name from way back. If I remember he carried an ivory-handled Colt."

Abigail's eyes went wide as she met the sheriff's.

Sheriff Murphy smiled. "That's him isn't it?"

"Valentine?" Stepping away from the desk, Abigail ran her hand through her hair. "No. The man I'm after called himself Cincinnati."

"Valentine. Cincinnati. Gunfighters have so many aliases it's impossible to keep track. His real name is probably something like *John Smith*."

"And he carries an ivory-handled Colt?"

The sheriff nodded. "If I remember right, Valentine—or Cincinnati as you call him—killed a bunch of people down in Durango a decade ago. Shot up a room full of cowboys and when the posse caught him he killed them all, too. It was big news at the time because a ten-year-old boy got caught in the crossfire. Died right there in the middle of the saloon."

Abigail stumbled backward, caught her balance on the wall and fell into one of the chairs. She thought of Beckett and what he'd said about his son Daniel. A man in Durango ten years ago had emptied his ivory-handled Colt into five men. His last bullet killed his son.

"He killed a boy?" Her voice was weak.

"Was the son of some cowboy ridin' through town. Kid happened to be in the wrong place at the wrong time and was gunned down by Mr. Valentine here. Why do you ask?"

The corners of Abigail's eyes slowly began to burn. She could feel tears welling up. "I know—" She cleared her throat. "I know his father."

"Jesus." Sheriff Murphy collapsed into his chair.

Abigail closed her eyes, caught her breath and calmed herself. After a moment, she opened them. "Where is he?"

The Sheriff sat up and gabbed the wire. "Says here he's on his way to Durango. Some marshal down that way put out the warrant and offered the reward."

Abigail pushed her hair behind her ears and sat up.

"Listen. I don't care if you've got to chase this asshole from here to hell and back, I want to help. Logan will be fine on its own for a few weeks."

Rubbing her hands on her legs, Abigail shook her head. "No." She stood. "I'm going after him alone. I owe it to my father, I owe it to Beckett … and I owe it to myself." She walked to the doorway and looked into the fresh twilight. "Duke Valentine needs to die."

TWENTY-EIGHT

THEY RODE to Silver Bow along a shallow creek that cut through a flat, dry prairie. The mountains they'd traveled all morning were now at least two dusty miles behind them. Nat maneuvered his mare alongside Beckett's sorrel to free himself of the dust cloud that had begun to engulf him.

Train tracks paralleled them ten yards north of the creek. To the east, across the low scrub brush of the prairie, sat Silver Bow. It appeared they were only a mile out and Nat could clearly see a large train depot surrounded by a smattering of small buildings.

Beckett had told him earlier that Butte City was only another seven miles east and served as a hub of leisure and entertainment for travelers, whereas Silver Bow was nothing more than a junction point between the east-west Northern Pacific and north-south Union Pacific lines.

As they neared the depot, Nat could see a sprawling train yard full of switch tracks and secondary lines that surrounded the large building. Past the yard, he saw a stagecoach heading in from the east, kicking up a large cloud of dust.

"Isn't much here is there?" Nat removed his hat and wiped his brow.

"Just the depot and a few whiskey shacks. Don't need much with Butte City so close."

Nat placed his hat back on his head. The midmorning sun was hot. It made him forget the cold they'd experienced in the mountains.

"Can't believe we're finally here." Nat turned in his saddle and looked back. Baxter was trotting along behind them. "Seems like it took us a lifetime to get through those mountains."

Beckett rubbed his bandaged flank and winced sharply.

"Your side bothering you?"

Quickly retrieving his hand, Beckett placed it back on his reins. "Ain't nothin'. Too much time in the saddle is all."

"You can say that again. Looking forward to a long nap on a soft train bench."

***

AFTER HITCHING the horses, Beckett stood next to the ticketing window behind an old couple who were apparently planning a trip to Chicago. They'd been talking to the ticket agent for over ten minutes asking every question possible. Beckett could tell the man behind the window was losing his patience.

Stepping to the edge of the platform, Beckett watched Nat toss a gnarled stick twenty yards out across the dusty prairie. Baxter tore off after it, pounced on and then picked up the piece of wood before bounding back. The sight made Beckett smile.

"Next." The ticket agent's voice echoed across the covered platform.

Beckett turned to see the old couple slowly walking away from the booth, tickets in hand. He stepped up and took their place. Leaning against the barred-window's frame with his sore left shoulder, he placed a handful of gold eagle coins on the counter.

"Durango."

The ticket agent looked at the money then up at Beckett. "Colorado?"

"Yes."

"We don't run to Durango."

Beckett watched as Baxter ran off into the distance after the stick. "Well, how close can you get me?"

The ticket agent let out an exaggerated sigh and pulled out a large schedule book. "Closest I can get you is—"

"Elijah!" A shrill voice boomed from deep inside the depot.

"Jesus Christ, woman," the ticket agent said to himself then turned and yelled back. "What?"

"Did you check in yesterday's shipment?"

"I ain't had time. Been dealing with goddamn customers all morning." The ticket agent looked up at Beckett. "Give me one second, okay?" He then turned and walked into the depot. "If you'd just get off my back for …" His voice trailed as he disappeared into the large building.

Beckett chuckled and looked around the ticket booth. It was very similar to the one in St. Regis but about twice as big. A telegraph machine sat on a table to the right, stacks of papers littered every surface and the walls were covered with maps and wanted posters. Beckett scanned them again out of habit. He didn't see his name. A clock on the left wall read 9:04.

It read 9:09 when the ticket agent returned. Mumbling to himself, he took a seat on his stool and looked up. "Okay. Where were you going? ... oh, right, Durango. We don't go to Durango."

"You were gonna to see how close you could get me."

"Right." The ticket agent again flipped open the large schedule book. "Let's see. The 10:25 to Grand Junction, Colorado will get you to, well, Grand Junction ... sometime around nine tomorrow morning." He ran his finger down the page. "From there you can transfer to Blackwater via the Denver and Rio Grande at 10:15. Get there sometime around noon. After that, you're on your own. There's a mining spur between Blackwater and Ironwood but I don't have that schedule. From there Durango is only about fifty miles or so."

"That'll have to do I guess." Beckett slid the money forward "Will that cover two tickets?"

"You want the transfer ticket to Blackwater as well?"

"Yes."

The ticket agent picked up three of the gold eagles and bounced them in his left hand.

"And I'll need access to the livestock car. We both have horses," Beckett added.

A THOUSAND YESTERDAYS

After picking up another coin, the ticket agent dropped them into a drawer and flipped open a box of printed tickets.

Beckett retrieved the remaining coins from the counter and slid them into his pocket.

"Alright. Four tickets. Two to Grand Junction. Two to Blackwater."

The ticket agent scribbled times and destinations in the appropriate spots on each ticket. After each one was filled out he slammed down a red stamp with some sort of intricate logo in the corner.

While he worked, a woman came into the booth from the back with a large roll of paper under her arm and a small hammer in her hand. Beckett assumed she was the owner of the shrill voice he'd heard earlier. She stood on her toes, pinned the upper left corner of the paper to the rear wall with a tack and hammered it in. She did the same to the upper right corner.

The ticket agent placed two tickets on the counter. "Here's the two for Grand Junction." He returned to finish the final tickets.

Beckett watched as the woman smoothed the long, curled piece of paper down the wall. As she placed a tack in the lower left corner, he saw what was printed across it.

REWARD
($10,000)
FOR THE CAPTURE, ALIVE OF ONE
DUKE VALENTINE
AGE, 35-40. HEIGHT, 6 FEET 3 INCHES. WEIGHT, 220 LBS.

BROWN HAIR, EVEN FEATURES. HAS A HEART-SHAPED
BRAND ON LOWER RIGHT ARM.
HE GUNNED DOWN MORE THAN TWELVE INNOCENT MEN
AND ONE YOUNG BOY IN COLD BLOOD.
THE ABOVE REWARD WILL BE PAID FOR HIS
ALIVE CAPTURE ONLY.

ZEBEDIAH CAIN—MARSHAL
IRONWOOD, COLORADO TERRITORY

No picture accompanied the text. Becket took a step back in shock. He looked down at his right arm. His heart-shaped brand was covered by his shirt.

"And here are the two for Blackwater." The ticket agent placed the final tickets on the counter.

"Elijah, did you see this? This fella's wanted for ten thousand dollars." The woman stood back and looked at the poster.

As the ticket agent turned to look, Beckett grabbed the tickets and hurried to the horses. He untied both, hopped onto his sorrel and led Nat's mare into the street.

"Looks like we've got some time to kill." Beckett handed the reins to Nat and looked over his shoulder. "Thinkin' we should head into Butte City for a drink."

"Sounds good to me." Nat mounted his mare. "How much time do we have?"

"Just enough." Beckett kicked his sorrel to a gallop.

TWENTY-NINE

ROBARGE SLID from his saddle and fell to his knees along the bank of a mountain stream. His Appaloosa dunked its nose into the cold water and slurped between breaths. He removed his leather coat and ammo belts and dropped them to the ground. Afterward he unbuttoned his shirt and slid it away from his left shoulder. The large bandage tied to his wound had not bled through. That was definitely a good sign.

The night of the thunderstorm Robarge had removed four lead balls from the black man's shotgun which were imbedded in his shoulder. After finding a dry alcove and building a fire, he dug out each lead ball with a small knife. Holding a clean bandage over the wounds, Robarge removed the barrel of his unloaded Colt from the embers of the fire and inserted its glowing red tip into the first hole. He howled as the flesh sizzled and smoked, took a breath and heated the barrel again. Amazingly he'd only passed out twice before finishing all four holes.

Now, he removed his hat, splashed water from the stream across his dusty, oily face and neck and drank. He'd forgotten how thirsty he'd been. After he filled his stomach with the cold mountain water, he sat back, untied the fabric that held the bandage against his shoulder and dropped it to the ground. He took a deep breath and peeled the bandage away. Its fibers stuck to the hardened scabs that surrounded each hole and stung as it broke away from them. The cool mountain air had a numbing effect as the wounds became exposed.

Robarge examined the damage. No swelling, no redness, no excess pain. He swiveled his left arm forward and back then out and in. Nothing but a dull ache. As he raised it up, though, a strong sharp pain shot through him and made him flinch. He quickly lowered his arm and leaned back.

Sun streaked through the trees and painted the stream with gold and orange. A warm breeze rustled the bushes and ruffled his hair. Robarge looked over his shoulder. He hadn't seen Holton or Quincey for over a day and doubted he'd ever see them again. Not that he'd miss them. After crossing the swollen river south of Missoula he'd pushed his Appaloosa to its limits and was thankful he rode such a young animal. Neither Holton or Quincey had mounts as strong.

When his horse was finished drinking and was nibbling on greens away from the stream, Robarge dressed, stood and hopped into his saddle. Turning his Appaloosa to the east, he kicked it to a gallop. Silver Bow was just over the next rise.

THIRTY

BECKETT SAT in the darkest corner of the saloon with his back to the wall. He'd made sure to enter the bar first so he could choose a seat without Nat's input or question. It had only taken them fifteen minutes to travel the seven miles from Silver Bow to Butte City and the first building they'd come across was the Butte City Inn and Saloon.

It reminded him of Doc Sherman's place in Temperance. The front corner was covered with large, curtained windows. A long, polished bar traversed the far left wall and tables filled the large room. This place even had a beat-up, old piano on a riser toward the back.

After sitting, Nat looked across at Beckett. "Think we probably need to go to the bar for our drinks."

Beckett sat up and looked at the gnarled old bartender perched on a stool. "Yeah. I suppose you're right."

Both men stood. Beckett held up his palm. "I'll get em. Gin?"

"You got it."

The room was mostly empty and only two other tables were occupied. At one was a pair of cowboys playing cards and at the other was a crimson-faced drunkard, passed out and snoring. Beckett looked beyond the piano to the stairs that led to rooms above. They were also unoccupied.

As he stepped up to the bar, he looked out through the batwings.

The grizzled bartender slid from his stool, grunted then hobbled across to him. "What'll it be?"

"What kind of beer you got back there?" Beckett's eyes didn't leave the front entrance.

"The kind that comes in a bottle."

"I'll take one of those and a tall glass of gin."

The bartender moved into Beckett's field of vision and looked across the room at Nat. He grumbled something under his breath.

"Would you mind if my friend played your piano?"

The bartender popped open the beer then filled a glass with gin. "Ain't too keen on a nigger bein' in my place."

Beckett reached into his pocket and pulled out five, ten-dollar gold eagles and slid them across the bar. He looked the bartender in the eye. "Don't really give a damn what you're keen on. Just want to hear my friend play the piano."

The bartender looked down at the coins and smiled. "Looks like you changed my mind. Your friend can play as long as he wants."

Beckett picked up the drinks. "Much obliged."

Returning to their table, he took a seat and slid the glass of gin across to Nat. Beckett took a swig from his beer bottle. It was surprisingly good. Not as good as the English ale he'd had at Doc Sherman's place but it would do.

"So, what are your plans?" Beckett looked at Nat but kept the entrance in his peripheral vision. "When we get to Colorado, I mean."

"Hadn't really thought of it." Nat took a drink. "How 'bout you? You haven't really said what you were going there for. Never seemed like a good time to ask."

Beckett pulled his attention away from the door for a moment. He looked down at his bottle. "My son died ten years ago. I'm going to see him."

Nat sat back in his chair. "Is that who the letter is for?"

Beckett looked up.

"I saw you obsessing over it when we were up on Sohon Pass." Nat took another drink. "You pull it out and look at it when you think I'm asleep."

Beckett smirked. "Yeah. That's who it's for. Had a whole stack I was gonna deliver to him before Cincinnati burned them in Cain's office." He took a swig and wiped the foam from his beard. "After I took care of Cincinnati and the sheriff I sat down and wrote another. It says everything I need to say."

"And after you deliver it?"

"Don't rightly know."

Nat finished his glass and sat back. "Think I'll give Denver a try. Hear it's a real progressive place. Maybe get a job in a kitchen somewhere."

"Why not the piano?"

Holding his hands up, Nat wiggled the remaining stumps of his pinkies. He'd changed the bandages the day before and they were still mostly white. "I think I'm done with the piano."

"I say that's bullshit. You still got eight good fingers."

Nat shook his head. "It would be like learning all over again."

Beckett signaled the bartender for another round knowing it would take him a while to deliver it. After a long couple of minutes of shuffling, the old man placed a fresh bottle in front of Beckett and a full glass in front of Nat.

"Would sure love to hear you play." The bartender said through yellow teeth to Nat. He turned and winked at Beckett then sauntered off.

"You tell him I play?"

"Just mentioned it." Beckett finished his first bottle. "He was real eager to hear what you could do."

Nat's eyes brightened. Beckett could almost see the wheels turning behind them.

"I don't know, Beckett."

"You *won't* know until you give it a shot."

Twisting in his chair, Nat looked back at the old bartender. "And the old man wants me to?"

"He's all kinds of excited. Real music fanatic I guess."

Nat sat in silence for a long moment and rubbed his hands. He picked up the full glass of gin, downed it and stood. "What the hell." He took off his bowler, placed it on the table and made his way to the piano.

Beckett pushed back his chair, picked up his second beer and followed.

Bending over, Nat pulled out the piano's bench, stepped over it and sat down. He stretched his remaining fingers, placed them over the ivory keys and plinked out a few notes. The piano was horribly out of tune. Eventually the notes turned into chords and then a melody. Within a minute Nat was hammering out an uptempo tune like he hadn't missed a beat.

Beckett flinched and touched his Bowie as the drunkard who'd been passed out across the room fell from his chair. He struggled up and danced, arms flailing as he stumbled between the tables.

Nat started to sing. "*Well, I went down south for to see my Sal. Polly wolly doodle al the day …*"

The men playing cards turned their attention to the piano. Both bobbed their heads. One whistled and cheered.

Nat continued. "*My Sal is a spunky gal. Polly wolly doodle all the day …*"

Beckett listened for a moment then walked toward the batwings.

The old bartender's attention was drawn to the piano. A large smile crossed his face. "Hot damn, your friend can play!"

Beckett downed the rest of his beer and placed the empty bottle on the bar. Pulling two of the four train tickets from his pocket, he confirmed that one was to Grand Junction and the other was to Blackwater. After a long look back at his friend, he tore them up and dropped them into a spittoon.

Making a detour to their table, Beckett removed a heavy leather pouch from his jacket and lifted Nat's bowler. He heard the metallic ring of gold coins as it landed on the hardwood. He dropped Nat's hat over it and slid through the batwings. From the street he heard: "*Behind the barn down on my knees. Polly wolly doodle all the day. I thought I heard a chicken sneeze. Polly wolly doodle all the day* ..."

Beckett mounted his sorrel and scanned the town—then the road to Silver Bow. No sign of lawmen. No sign of a posse. No sign of anyone.

As he turned his horse back toward the train depot, Baxter came bounding to him.

"Go on. Git!" Beckett snapped at the dog.

Baxter sat and stirred the dust with his stump, tongue flapping anxiously.

Beckett kicked his sorrel and continued west. The dog followed.

"No." He slid from his saddle and stomped in the dog's direction. "Get out of here." He clapped his hands and kicked dirt. "Go find Nat. Neither of you is safe with me."

Baxter scurried away.

As Beckett grasped his saddle horn to mount, the mutt slinked back, mouth closed, ears curious.

Grabbing a large stone, Beckett ran at the dog and threw it. The rock landed with a puff in front of the animal. "Go on!" He yelled. "Go find Nat."

Baxter took off across the prairie.

Beckett watched the dog for a moment, mounted his sorrel and kicked it west. He looked back after a while to see Baxter sitting alert outside the entrance of the Butte City Inn and Saloon. He could still hear Nat's melody echoing from inside.

THIRTY-ONE

ROBARGE KICKED his Appaloosa to a gallop when he saw the train. It was sitting idle alongside the depot across the dusty prairie. Steam billowed from its smokestack. His horse struggled to keep the fast pace. Many days of hard riding had taken its toll on the poor animal.

As he approached the depot, he veered north to arrive behind the line of train cars. He didn't want Valentine to see him if he was aboard. Robarge rode past the last car and around to the ticketing window on the far side of the depot. The train was still idling. Still belching steam.

He jumped from his saddle and ran to the barred window. No one was inside.

"Hey!" Robarge reached in between the bars and rapped against the wall with his open hand. "Anyone there?"

A moment later a uniformed ticket agent entered. "I'd appreciate it if you would retrieve your arm, sir."

Seeing a large wanted poster with Valentine's name on it against the far wall, Robarge pointed. "That man. Duke Valentine. Have you seen him? Is he on that train?"

"If you remove your arm I'd be happy to answer your question."

Robarge grit his teeth and slid his arm from between the bars. "Is he on that train?" His tone was urgent.

"Haven't seen a fella with a heart-shaped brand on his arm if that's what you're askin'." The ticket agent looked back at the sign. "Never seen a reward that big before. Thought it was a misprint."

Robarge took a breath. "Have you seen a tall man with a beard and a sheepskin coat? Carries a big Bowie knife on his hip. Was heading to Durango."

The ticket agent's eyes widened. "Yes. I've seen *him*. Came through here this morning."

"Is he on that train?"

"You tellin' me the fella with the beard is Duke Valentine?"

"Is-he-on-that-train?!" Robarge's voice boomed.

"This one? No. The fella you're talkin' about took the 10:25 to Grand Junction. Headin' to Blackwater after that. Told him we don't run to Durango."

Robarge looked at the clock above the ticket agent's head—3:20. He stepped away from the window and looked to the south. A weight lifted from his shoulders but a tightness formed in his belly. He turned back to the window.

"Where is this train heading?"

"Salt Lake."

"When does it leave?"

"3:35. It's runnin' early for a change."

"Get me to Blackwater." Robarge placed some cash on the counter. "Your telegraph work?"

"Sure does."

"Give me a pen and paper. I want to send a wire."

ZEBEDIAH STRUCK A MATCH and lit his freshly-rolled cigarette. The flame flared and the paper crackled as he inhaled. Throwing the spent match into the dirt, he exhaled and watched as his men gathered around.

The Korrigan brothers sat at his flanks—Thaddeus on a sun-bleached black to his right and Reuben on a beautiful white Arabian to his left. The latter brother pushed shells into his Winchester's polished brass receiver. Across from them in a semicircle were six hard-looking men riding horses of varying grays and browns.

The man in their center was Hank "Sockeye" Smith. Zebediah had arrested him three years earlier for the rape and murder of four women—one of whom was a nun. After discovering his deadly-accurate precision with a long-rifle, Marshal Cain decided that with Smith's talents, he would be more valuable as an employee than a five hundred dollar bounty.

Sockeye wore dark chaps, a long, black cotton duster and a ragged hat. He had a Remington at his side and a long-barrel Spencer in a saddle holster. In his boot was a short blade knife he used to "seduce" his female conquests.

The remaining men were rough-looking and well-armed. Zebediah had never worked with any of them but doubted that Sockeye would hire anybody but seasoned, professional killers.

Zebediah took another pull on his cigarette and exhaled. "I understand you've all been briefed on the situation."

The men did not answer. They just stared back awaiting instructions.

"Valentine is en route to Durango. If he is not there already, we will meet him." Zebediah leaned forward against his saddle horn. "He-is-*mine*. If you kill him first …" He took another puff then exhaled. "… you will be next. Are we clear?"

The men nodded.

"Wing him, beat him, I don't care. Just bring him to me alive." He looked to his right. "Reuben."

Reuben Korrigan eased his Arabian a step forward and spoke to the men. "We ride south through the night. It's three days to Durango. I want to be there in two. Now, if we—"

"Marshal Cain." A voice echoed down the street. "Wait."

The small, round man who ran the Ironwood train depot's telegraph ran down the center of the street toward them. He had a folded piece of paper in his hand. Sliding to a stop in front of Zebediah, he placed his hands on his knees and panted. Between breaths he spoke.

"A wire … just came through … from Mister Robarge."

Zebediah reached out. The fat man caught his breath and handed over the paper. Unfolding it, he read the telegraph operator's eight handwritten words.

Valentine on train to Blackwater. Arr. noon tomorrow.

Zebediah smiled, folded the paper and addressed his men. "Slight change of plans." He dropped the paper to the ground. "We're heading back to Blackwater."

"Sir …" The fat telegraph operator was still panting. "… the last train to Blackwater just left. Won't be another until tomorrow afternoon."

Zebediah took a final draw from his cigarette and threw the smoking butt into the dirt.

"Then we ride."

AFTER LOADING his Appaloosa in the livestock car, Robarge walked to the head of the train and stepped aboard. The first car was full, as was the second. When he reached the third, he found an empty set of seats toward the back. He removed the shotgun holster from his back and his gun belts, placed them in the overhead compartment and sat down.

For a moment Robarge looked out the window at the mountains he'd come down earlier then turned his gaze to the passenger across from him. He was instantly taken aback by what he saw.

The young woman's long legs were covered with freshly oiled, leather chaps. A thin white blouse showed hints of a supple bosom and a new, flat-brimmed hat hid her shimmering auburn hair. On the empty seat next to her lay a thick vest made of what looked like black bear and on her hips were two pearl-handled, double-action Colt Thunderers. The same model as the skull encrusted one at his side.

"Howdy, miss." He removed his hat and tipped his head. After replacing it he chuckled. "What are you—some kind of bounty hunter?"

The woman looked up at him. Her eyes were a jewel-green like he'd never seen before.

"Sure. I guess you could call me that."

PART THREE

THE GUNFIGHTER

THIRTY-TWO

CINCINNATI STOOD over Beckett with a red-hot branding iron in his pale, bloody left hand. In his right was his ivory-handled Colt. Centered on the tie around his neck was his large, crimson ruby pin. Sun filtered through its facets and made it glow like the depths of hell. The top of the dead deputy's head was completely missing, yet his lower jaw with its shattered teeth still was able to speak.

"Why did you kill me?" Cincinnati's voice was clear despite his missing upper jaw. "I wanted to be you."

He raised his Colt, cocked the hammer and pulled the trigger.

Beckett's left shoulder exploded in a cloud of red.

He felt no pain.

Reaching over with his right hand, he covered the large wound and felt cold blood bubble through his fingers.

"Was I not good enough?" Cincinnati cocked the hammer again. "I was fast. I used the right gun." He pulled the trigger.

The bullet went through Beckett's right hand and into his shoulder.

Still no pain.

His left arm seemed to be on the verge of separating from his body.

Cincinnati placed his boot on Beckett's cheek and slowly pushed his head to the left. Beckett followed the movement with his body until he was lying on his side.

Abby stood five feet away. Her hands were bloody, her dress torn. She didn't move.

Beckett opened his mouth to call out to her but no sound came.

Cincinnati raised the brand. Its glowing heart-shaped end sizzled in the breeze. "I wanted to be you."

Beckett could smell the fabric of his shirt singe as Cincinnati placed the brand against his right flank.

Now, there was pain.

Immense pain.

Pain he'd felt only once before.

Beckett tried to turn away but his body was frozen. He tried to scream but still no sound came. The brand sizzled loudly against his skin. The air was filled with the smell of burning flesh.

"I wanted to be you!" Cincinnati pushed the glowing red metal in harder.

Beckett's right flank was on fire.

Abby just stood there. Her arms were limp. Thick blood streamed from her fingers to the dirt.

"I wanted to be—"

A THOUSAND YESTERDAYS

BECKETT WOKE with a start.

His legs shot out and slammed against the seat in front of him. When he slowly realized where he was, he eased up and looked around. Seated on the last bench of the train's rear passenger car, he could see heads bounce and sway in rows ahead of him. As he focused his eyes, a dark, cloaked head rose from the seat he'd kicked.

"Are you alright?" An old woman wearing a hooded nun's cassock turned and peered over her seat-back.

Beckett didn't know. His head was warm, his shirt was soaked and his right flank burned. He realized he'd been grabbing it with his left hand making the pain more intense so he let go and straightened himself.

"Yeah. I'm fine."

"You look like you might be coming down with something." The old nun's eyes were a pale, ice blue. "You're white as a sheet." She reached out to touch his forehead.

Beckett pushed her hand away. "I said I'm fine."

The nun was quiet for a moment then nodded and sat back down.

Beckett took a deep breath and ran his fingers through his damp hair. His forehead was wet and warm. His right hand trembled as it crossed his vision. Clenching it into a fist, he rubbed it with his left.

The pain from the shotgun wound on his flank was worsening. He gingerly touched his side then flinched. Without looking, he knew that the skin around each lesion was turning red. Soon it would spread to the rest of his side. Why hadn't he stopped to clean the wound earlier? Why had he kept running? There was not much he could do now but wait out the fever and hope that would be the worst of it.

As he looked out the window, he studied the small passing town. The last building in a row of seven was the Emberville Post Office and General Store. Blackwater was only another five miles away. It could be a good place to stop and heal as long as the wanted posters hadn't made it that far. There had been none in Grand Junction.

Leaning his head back, he stared at the curved ceiling. Long, cherry-stained boards ran the length of the car. Freshly-painted white trim framed them on either side just above the windows. He closed his eyes and thought of Abigail. Not the bloody, wordless Abigail from his dreams but the beautiful, innocent Abigail he'd met a week earlier.

As he dozed off, the brakes squealed and the train car lurched forward. His saddlebag slid from the bench next to him and onto the floor. Had he fallen asleep? After the train came to a complete stop, Beckett pivoted in his seat and looked out the window toward the rear. Emberville's last building was only a quarter-mile back. As he turned and scanned the car, passengers around him stood and milled.

The nun who'd reached for his forehead spoke to a man across the aisle. "Are we there already?"

The man shrugged.

Beckett wasn't aware of a town between Emberville and Blackwater. He checked that his Bowie was still at his side and stood. Looking out his window, he saw mostly sagebrush and dust, framed by dark mountains miles to the north. A lone church stood just ten yards from the train's last freight car. The building was severely lit by the high, midday sun and aging ivory paint peeled and crumbled from its disheveled facade.

Turning, he looked down the train to the east. The track had begun to veer to the south so his view of the engine was obscured. From what he could see, there was no sign of road agents. No sign of a lawman.

Beckett stepped across the aisle, slid into the empty seat and peered out the opposite window. Three freight cars and a caboose were behind them to the west. Again, nothing but sagebrush and dust in the distance. As he turned to the front, he tensed and his adrenaline surged. The track ahead of them curved south and allowed him a view of the front of the train and the engine.

Nine hard-looking men sat on horseback a few yards down the track. The tallest two—they could have been brothers—slid from their saddles and walked up to the engine. One of them pointed a old Winchester Yellow Boy at the engineer.

Their leader was an imposing man wearing a dusty, flat-brimmed burgundy hat and a marshal's badge. The hat was identical to the one that had rolled down the street in Temperance after Beckett had blown the top off of Sheriff Walter Cain's head.

The rider with the badge spoke to his men then waved one of them around to the north side of the train. He led the remaining five down the southern side where Beckett now stood. Their horses looked tired and weary. When they reached the first car, one of the riders dismounted and stepped up to the outside door.

Beckett shook his head to clear it, closed his eyes and willed the pain in his flank to subside—if only temporarily. He then stepped back across the aisle, picked up his saddlebag and quietly slipped out the rear door of the car.

THIRTY-THREE

STEAM HISSED from the idling engine's large pistons and drifted between Zebediah and the Korrigan brothers who were in the process of detaining the engineer.

"Valentine could be on this train." Zebediah turned his roan and spoke to Sockeye and his men. He could feel the horse panting beneath him. It had been a hard, over-night ride from Ironwood. "I want a man in each one of these passenger cars. Check everybody. Valentine was last described as a mountain man so look for someone tall—possibly with a beard. He's dangerous. I don't want any fuck-ups." He pointed at a long-haired, barrel-chested man called Walcott. "Head around the other side and make sure he doesn't run. If you see him, yell. Do not kill him."

Walcott nodded and turned his horse.

Zebediah led everyone else down the southern side of the train. When they reached the first passenger car, one of Sockeye's men dismounted, unholstered his revolver and pulled open the outside door. He stepped inside and slowly made his way down the isle.

As Walcott walked his horse down the opposite side of the train, Zebediah had a difficult time marking his progress. The high sun cast a dark shadow under the cars and about a yard out on the north side. If it wasn't for the fact each hoof was capped in white hair, Zebediah wouldn't have been able to discern Walcott's gray gelding in the dark shadow.

While Zebediah watched Walcott pass between the first two cars, another one of Sockeye's men dismounted and stepped inside the second car. Zebediah scanned the stunned and curious faces in the windows. Most were probably miners on their way to Eureka and Ironwood looking for work and a possible fortune.

When they reached the gap between the second and third car, there was no sign of Walcott. As he leaned over in his saddle and looked west beneath the train, Zebediah caught sight of the distinctive, white-crested hooves of Walcott's horse nearing the fourth and last passenger car.

BECKETT KNELT on the metal platform behind the last passenger car. Perforated steps led down from both sides and a brass railing encircled the ledge above the large coupler. The roof of the car extended over the platform bathing it in a dark shadow that starkly contrasted the harsh brightness of the sunlight that baked the front wall of the freight car across the coupled divide.

On the door Beckett had exited was a small window covered with a thin, green curtain. A gap on either side allowed him a view into the car and out the long row of windows along both sides. The riders had yet to appear on the south side but on the north a thick man was making his way at an even pace, his long mop of hair billowing in the soft breeze. A Springfield rifle was in his left hand.

The last three cars in line were freight cars which had no access doors on the end like the passenger cars. The only way in was through one of the two large sliding doors, one on either side. Both doors were in plain view of either the man with the marshal's badge coming from the south or the man with the long hair quickly approaching from the north. Beckett's sorrel was in the last of the three freight cars, the one just before the caboose.

Placing his hand on his Bowie, Beckett weighed his options. He made his decision when he saw the gray snout of the thick man's horse. As the Springfield came into view, Beckett reached for it with both hands, twisting it from the man's grasp then thrust the stock into the man's throat, crushing his voice box before he could yell. When the thick man instinctively grabbed at his neck, he yanked the reins, stopping the horse. Beckett reared back and drove the end of the gun into the man's temple. With a muffled crack he could feel his skull shatter. The big man's eyes rolled back into his head and his arms fell to his side. Before he could tip out of his saddle, Beckett reached over, grabbed the thick man's long hair and laid him forward against the saddle horn. Grabbing the reins, Beckett straddled the horse behind its dead rider, slid the rifle into its side holster and threw his saddlebag over his shoulder.

He could feel the animal's tired legs give slightly from the added weight but kicked it forward anyway. Peering back over his shoulder through the two sets of windows he saw the man with the marshal's badge reach the fourth passenger car just as Beckett disappeared behind the first freight car.

AS SOCKEYE'S FOURTH MAN, an Indian called Ahote, hopped down from his mount and stepped into the last passenger car, Thaddeus Korrigan rode up beside Zebediah.

"Reuben has the engineer under control, Zeb." He ran his thumb and forefinger over his mustache wiping away dirt and sweat. "No sign of Valentine?"

Zebediah watched as Sockeye positioned his horse next to one of the last windows of the car, removed his ragged hat and bowed to the old nun inside. The confused woman smiled tentatively. Sockeye then pursed his lips, kissed the air and flicked his long, pointed tongue at her. The woman's blue eyes widened as she turned away in disgust.

"No. No sign of Valentine," Zebediah answered. "If he's not on this train he must be back in Grand Junction."

"Could be in one of them freight cars."

"I don't see how. There's no way into them except by the side doors. He couldn't have gotten in without us or Walcott seeing him."

Zebediah looked back to the first three cars. Two of the men who'd searched them were already mounted and heading over. The third exited his car and shook his head.

"Mister Cain." Ahote's voice came from the rear platform of the fourth car. "Valentine is not here."

BECKETT REACHED OVER, pulled the bolt and flipped open the latch. The large door to the third and last freight car was suspended by two flat hooks that rode along a slider. Fresh, black grease dripped from where it had been recently applied to the long metal bar. Leaning over, he grabbed the thin, wrought iron handle, held his breath and slowly pushed the door open.

At first there was some resistance but soon he found that it moved easily and with relatively little sound. He hoped the constant hiss of steam from the engine would mask any noise the large door made. When the opening was big enough for him to squeeze through, he tied the thick man's horse to the wrought iron handle, secured the body and hopped down inside.

The freight car was mostly empty. Streaks of sunlight cut through the dusty air from thin, horizontal slits in the siding. Beckett's sorrel, the lone animal in the car, was tied to a hitch at the eastern, engine end. Walking over he stroked its mane, whispered in its ear and peered through one of the horizontal openings.

The man with the badge neared the south side of the second freight car and stopped. He yelled something to one of his men who dismounted, flipped the latch and slid open the door to the first freight car. Two of the others joined him in searching it.

Beckett threw his saddlebag onto his sorrel, untied the reins and led it to the door. As he stopped to push it open far enough to fit his horse, his eyes caught something stacked against the far west end.

Next to five wooden crates were three familiar metal barrels. He took a step closer and confirmed his suspicions. Turning, he saw through one of the thin slits at the far end of the car that the men were now opening the second freight car and hopping inside. Beckett ran his hand across the stamped logo on the end of one of the barrels, pulled a box of matches from his pocket and smiled.

THIRTY-FOUR

"**NOTHING HERE, SIR.**" One of Sockeye's men jumped down from the second freight car.

Thaddeus Korrigan unholstered his right Scofield and spun it. "Maybe you're right, Zeb. Maybe he's not in them freight cars."

Zebediah watched as the three men made their way to the final car. The Indian, Ahote, waited with his hand on his revolver.

"What's the plan if he ain't here?" Thaddeus spun the revolver in triplets, forward then back, forward then back. "We ridin' to Grand Junction?"

Sockeye positioned his horse a few yards from the door of the third freight car and held his Remington at the ready as he'd done with the previous two.

Thaddeus slid his left Scofield from its holster and spun it in concert with the right—but in the opposite direction. Back then forward, back then forward. "I ain't never been to Grand Junction. Hear they got Mormons there. Not as many as Salt Lake but I hear they got 'em."

Zebediah leaned over in his saddle and looked for Walcott's horse. Just below the far door of the third freight car, shuffled the white-crested hooves of his gray gelding.

Completely focused on his Scofields, Thaddeus increased the speed of his spinning. "Hear them Mormon gals are great in the sack. Hear you can have as many—"

"Would you please shut the fuck up and stop that goddamned spinning?"

Thaddeus dropped his guns into their holsters.

After a beat, Zebediah turned his horse and positioned himself out beyond Sockeye so he could have a clear view of the freight car's door. Thaddeus followed.

One of the men pulled the bolt from the clasp and flipped open the latch. As he slid the large door open, a brilliant light shone from inside. Zebediah could see the worn facade of a white church through the open far door of the car. Above it, perched atop its modest steeple, was a lackluster, bronze cross.

As Zebediah reached for his Merwin Hulbert, the brilliant glow from the inside of the car instantly became infinitely brighter.

The massive explosion began as a glowing ball of fire. It expanded and tore the freight car apart from the inside, board-by-board.

The man who'd opened the door was immediately vaporized and the two who had followed him were blown into fragments of flesh, blood and flying body parts.

A concussion wave followed, knocking Sockeye and Ahote from their horses. Thaddeus and Zebediah fell a moment later.

A THOUSAND YESTERDAYS

As Zebediah hit the ground, the world faded. All sound was silenced and time seemed to stand still. When he finally regained his senses the heat of a towering fireball forced him back to the ground. The ringing and pressure in his ears was unbearable.

Collecting as much will as possible, Zebediah stood and turned toward the train. The third freight car no longer existed. The force of the explosion had sent the blackened caboose cruising westward down the track. Half of the second freight car was gone and both it and the first had been derailed and toppled into the dust and sagebrush. Screaming passengers climbed from shattered windows and poured out of the open doors of their cars.

Zebediah shook his head to clear it. The ringing in his ears was so pervasive he could barely think. Thaddeus stumbled to him and gestured with one of his Scofields toward the church. Zebediah nodded and agreed that Valentine was either inside or behind the now blackened old building.

As Zebediah tried to stand, Reuben Korrigan rode over, slid from his saddle and helped him up. The clean-shaven Korrigan brother had been far enough from the explosion that he was barely affected.

Sockeye Smith stumbled from where he'd landed. He rubbed his hands over his cheeks and looked down at the blood that had been seeping from his ears.

"I can't hear." He touched them again. "I'm deaf." There was panic in his voice. He slammed his palms against his ears. "I'm fucking deaf!"

"Get the horses." Zebediah was relieved he could still hear his own voice over the ringing in his ears. He pushed away from Reuben. "Get Valentine!"

Zebediah's roan was pacing in a circle a few yards away, shaking its head as if it had water in its ears. He collected the reins and hopped on. It took a few strong kicks to get the confused animal to focus and head back toward his men.

Ahote lay in the dirt near where he'd been before the explosion. His left arm was gone and his left leg was a mangled mess. Crawling and clawing away from the disfigured remains of his horse, he coughed up blood. "Help me! Please!"

As the Korrigan brothers collected their horses and readied themselves, Zebediah rode over to the pleading Indian, pulled his Merwin Hulbert and pointed it at his head.

"Please, Mister Cain. Help—"

Zebediah pulled the trigger.

Sockeye was still in shock, kneeling and holding his ears. Reuben collected the man's horse and led it over to him. As soon as he saw the animal, Sockeye reached out and pulled his Spencer rifle from its saddle holster. Pointing into the crowd of fleeing passengers, he screamed in anger and fired.

His first shot downed a man in a pin-striped suit, his second toppled a miner and his third took the top off of a young Mexican's head.

Panting, he dropped his rifle.

Zebediah rode around into Sockeye's field of view and pointed his gun. "Get on your horse."

Sockeye understood the command even though it was obvious he couldn't hear. Zebediah could see the man's panic and anger turn into a focused fury. He picked up his rifle and mounted his ride.

Zebediah turned his roan toward the old church.

"Let's get that son of a bitch."

THIRTY-FIVE

RUN OR FIGHT? Neither was a favorable option. As the wind whistled past his ears, Beckett struggled with the question that required an immediate answer.

He had kicked his sorrel to a gallop as soon as he felt the explosion. It hadn't taken much to get the animal to move. The old church had provided ample protection from the blast. There was only a minor ring in his ears.

His infected flank was a different story. With every hoof-fall it felt as if the Cincinnati of his dreams was pressing in his red-hot branding iron harder. Gritting his teeth against the pain, Beckett looked behind to see the man with the badge stand up and try to regain control of the situation. Passengers flooded from the train cars and helped shield Beckett's escape east along the tracks.

A few moments later, he heard a gunshot. Then two more. The short, hairy man seemed to be shooting passengers at random. Beckett ducked and pushed his sorrel harder.

Run or fight? The long-haired man was dead from a cracked skull and the explosion should have eliminated at least three more of them. That left the marshal and three or four of his men. All of whom would be struggling with the aftermath of being in close proximity to a huge, black-powder explosion. Their horses were also noticeably overworked and in no shape to keep up with his well-rested sorrel.

Running would only temporarily solve the problem, though. Within a day, his infection would begin to impair his ability to ride and within two, he'd have no choice but to rest and recuperate. Assuming the fever didn't kill him, he'd need nearly a week to recover before he could continue, leaving plenty of time for four or five well-armed and now very angry men to track him down. Running would be slow suicide but turning back and fighting them out in the open would be no better.

As he continued along the tracks he looked for a suitable ambush location. There was still nothing but dust and sagebrush in every direction. Dark mountains that would provide ideal cover loomed twenty miles to the north but the marshal and his men would likely catch up before he could reach them. With his strength already waning, Beckett had no choice but to take care of his pursuers as soon as possible. That was the only real option.

Before long, the mining town of Blackwater emerged on the horizon. Its many buildings were situated on three parallel streets that ran south from the train depot. The farthest east was Harrison Street, in the center was Main Street and the western most was Patterson Street. As he got closer, Beckett could see many side avenues and alleys tucked between the buildings. On the outskirts were houses and toward the south end of town was a makeshift camp made up of tents, lean-tos and huts.

Beckett turned past the train depot and down Main Street. When he saw the sidewalks were lined with people—many of whom were women and children—he reined his horse to a dusty stop. A large, hand-painted banner above him read:

> FOURTH ANNUAL BLACKWATER
> HARVEST FESTIVAL AND PARADE
> SUNDAY, SEPTEMBER 27TH.

As Beckett counted the days in his head trying to recall the current date he heard the crack of a drum followed by the sound of dueling bugles coming from the east. A moment later, a small group of school-aged girls wearing yellow dresses came marching around the corner throwing daisy pedals from white baskets. Beckett backed his sorrel out of their way and turned it toward Harrison, the easternmost street. A large parade was heading north in his direction and was in the process of making a u-turn south down Main Street.

Behind the flower girls was a group of young boys leading various farm animals. One of the smallest children struggled to pull an uncooperative goat. When Beckett looked down the parade line, he saw the source of the music.

"Shit. The goddamned cavalry?"

Eight soldiers wearing their dress-blues and riding atop freshly brushed horses brought up the rear of the parade. A small drum and bugle corps led them on foot.

"Shit," Beckett said again.

Turning his sorrel, he led it back around the north side of the train depot. An old woman wearing a large hat sat on the lone bench, waiting for a train that was already late.

"Those army boys sure are loud." She looked up at Beckett as he passed. "Must have been practicing their shooting down that way earlier." She pointed to the west. "Sounded like a cannon went off."

Beckett ignored the woman and rode on. He stopped when he saw a plume of dust being kicked up by a group of riders in the distance. The marshal and his men were moving exceptionally fast despite their obviously tired horses.

"Shit," Beckett said a third time.

"Excuse me?" The old woman turned away in disgust.

Beckett contemplated the current course of events, adjusted his plan accordingly and rode back into town.

THIRTY-FIVE

"**SHIT. IT'S THE CAVALRY.**" Thaddeus Korrigan holstered his Scofield, lowered his hat and turned his sun-bleached black away from the uniformed men on horseback. "What we gonna do, Zeb?"

Letting his roan catch its breath, Zebediah took a moment to analyze the situation. "Valentine's here. I know it." He removed his father's burgundy hat and ran a hand trough his hair. "He'll use the parade to his advantage. Thad, ride down Harrison. Reuben, you take Patterson." He replaced the hat. "I'll head down Main Street on foot."

Sockeye pulled a bloody finger from his ear and shook his head. Zebediah snapped his fingers to get his attention. "Hey …" He jabbed Sockeye in the chest and yelled. "… ride to the end of town. If you see Valentine …" Zebediah unholstered his Merwin Hulbert and mimed firing it into the air. "Got it?"

Nodding his head, Sockeye yelled, "If I see him I'll …" He pulled his Remington and mimicked the gesture.

Holstering his revolver, Zebediah traced the scar on his right hand. "This man is dangerous. I've seen what he can do." He slid from his saddle. "Do not underestimate him."

Thaddeus and Reuben both nodded. Sockeye had a bewildered look. He drilled a finger into his other ear.

"No matter what, bring him to me alive."

The Korrigan brothers turned their horses and headed down their assigned streets. Following their lead, Sockeye kicked his horse to a gallop and circled around to the south side of town.

The army cavalry had just finished rounding the corner as Zebediah stepped up onto Main Street's eastern sidewalk. As he made his way behind the line of onlookers at a quick pace, he scanned the crowd for a face he hadn't seen for ten years. He kept his Merwin Hulbert holstered but rested his right palm on the grip.

THADDEUS KORRIGAN led his horse down Harrison Street. Pushing back his duster, he slid his left Scofield from its holster and spun it. As muscle memory kicked in, the practiced movement instantly calmed his nerves. Even though the ringing had mostly disappeared, his ears still felt as if they were full of water. Reflexively, he moved his jaw up and down in an exaggerated motion trying to get his ears to crackle and pop.

After the parade passed their location, people cleared the sidewalks and slowly made their way through alleys and between buildings to Main Street where the parade had continued. Only a few stragglers remained. Passing the Blackwater Gambling Hall, Thaddeus removed his hat and bowed to the scantly clad whores who whistled from its upstairs balcony. One of the more sizable ladies slipped a pale, doughy breast from her bodice, bounced it in her hand and kissed the air in his direction. Thaddeus smiled.

A few yards away was a food wagon with brightly-painted signs that advertised hot, German meat pies and potato cakes. Instantly Thaddeus' stomach reminded him that he hadn't eaten in over twenty-four hours. When he saw that the merchant was in the process of packing up his wares, Thaddeus spun his revolver into its holster, looked back to make sure Zebediah was nowhere in sight and hopped down from his sun-bleached black.

"Whoa there, mister. I'll take one of them meat pies."

The merchant ceased what he was doing, acknowledged Thaddeus with a nod and wrapped a pie in brown paper.

"Two bits."

Thaddeus handed over a few coins and took the pie. "Much obliged."

The thick, meat-filled pastry wasn't hot like the sign had advertised but Thaddeus didn't mind. As he took a bite, grease ran down his chin and onto his shirt.

"Damn."

Before he could clean himself up, Thaddeus saw a large figure abruptly disappear into the shadows behind the adjacent building.

The merchant continued packing. "Ain't you worried about missing the—"

Thaddeus held up a finger to silence the man, unholstered his revolvers and stepped toward the shadows.

A THOUSAND YESTERDAYS

PATTERSON STREET was almost completely deserted. Reuben Korrigan kicked his white Arabian to a moderate gait and scanned the empty doorways and alleys on either side of the road. He could hear the drum and bugle corps' mediocre rendition of "Glory, Hallelujah" echoing between the buildings.

With everyone congregating around the festivities one street to the east, the sidewalks around him were mostly empty. To the left, a black man swept the walk in front of the town's general store. Across from him was the livery where a tall woman wearing chaps and a riding outfit was brushing down a light-colored quarter horse. Reuben tipped his hat in passing but received only a sideways glance in return as the woman continued her work.

When he reached the midpoint of the street, he reined his horse to a stop. On a bench in front of one of the town's saloons lay a tall man with a hat over his face. Each time his chest rose he let out a loud snore.

SOCKEYE TESTED his left ear one last time by inserting a finger and removing it. Nothing. It was completely dead of hearing. His right ear was only slightly better. He could barely make out the sound of his own heart beating through the steady hissing in his ear. When he snapped his fingers next to his head, only a muffled thud broke through the hiss.

"Goddam asshole." His voice reverberated through his skull but was only slightly audible on his right side.

Leading his horse through a makeshift mining camp at the south end of Blackwater, Sockeye marveled at the number of ramshackle tents Valentine could be hiding in. The only thing more futile than searching them all would be to search the entire town. Positioning himself at the end of Main Street with the parade heading directly for him, he could just make out Zebediah in the crowd.

"Fucking waste of time." He again spoke to himself but the words were no clearer. "We ain't gonna find him here, Zeb." Reflexively he beat the side of his head as if to clear water from his right ear. "If he is here at all."

Sockeye let out a long sigh then turned and rode to a large Catholic church at the end of Harrison Street. Next to it was a long, lean-to stable. For a moment he contemplated taking a break to visit one of the lovely, cloaked ladies inside. He reached over, slid his fingers down into his boot and confirmed his skinning knife was still there. It had been a long time since he'd been with a woman.

As he peered into one of the church's windows, something in the adjacent stable caught his eye. Each of the open-faced building's five stalls were absent of animals except for one at the nearest end where a tired, chestnut sorrel stood nibbling on hay. There was nothing strange about a horse in a stable. However, this one was still saddled and breathing heavily. Sockeye stopped to investigate.

Sliding from his horse, he approached the animal, his hand on his Remington. A tear-drop shaped leather bag hung from the rear of the saddle. Since he was no longer able to hear approaching footsteps, he periodically looked over his shoulder. There was no sign of anyone around.

Sockeye pulled open the mouth of the bag and reached inside. The first thing his hand touched was small wooden box. He removed it, flipped up its brass latch and opened it. The old cigar container smelled of sweet tobacco and contained an ink pen, some paper and a book of matches. Rifling through it he found that the folded papers were blank and that the box contained nothing of value. He dropped the container and its contents into the hay.

Looking over his shoulder again, he reached back into the bag. This time his hand touched something more puzzling. He grasped what felt like a wax-covered stick and removed it. As soon as he saw what it was he quickly and carefully placed it back inside and felt around. He jerked his hand out when he realized the entire bottom half of the bag was full of dynamite.

Sockeye pulled his Remington and spun around. There was still no sign of anyone. He stepped back from the horse and moved down the rest of the long stable, checking each stall one by one, gun first. As he neared the last, he saw what looked like a body crouched in the corner. Sockeye slowly cocked the hammer and stepped closer.

ZEBEDIAH HAD BEEN outpacing the parade and was now almost even with the drum and bugle corps. As he neared the center of Main Street, he heard Thaddeus call from Harrison. His voice echoed through a narrow alley that joined the two streets.

"Zeb, we got him!"

Zebediah pulled his Merwin Hulbert and turned down the narrow street. There was no sign of Thaddeus on the other side. From around the corner he heard another call.

"We got Valentine!"

THIRTY-SEVEN

"I STILL CAN'T BELIEVE we're after the same man." He dropped his bullet belts onto the bench across from Abigail and sat down. After placing his holstered sawed-off on top of them, he looked at her. "You sure you don't mind me sitting with you again?" Leaning forward, he acted as if he was ready to leave at her command.

"Sit wherever you want."

The man Abigail had met on the train in Silver Bow had introduced himself as Beau Robarge and insisted she call him by his first name. After he'd complemented her on her unique attire and her choice in sidearms, he'd asked where she was heading. A few questions later they realized they were both after a man called Valentine. They spent most of the rest of the trip to Salt Lake City in silence. Abigail hadn't been able to take her mind off of poor Garrett or the revelation that Cincinnati had killed Beckett's son.

Now, twenty hours later, Beau and Abigail sat across from each other in another train car waiting to get on their way to Grand Junction.

"You survive that hotel last night?" Beau reached over the top of his head with his right hand and pulled until his neck popped.

"I've slept in worse." She looked out the window at Salt Lake City's expansive train yard.

"Couldn't have been as bad as the hard dirt they got here." He pushed his jaw to the right and his spine cracked again. "I've slept on actual rock that was softer."

Abigail smiled to herself and watched as two workers lowered a water tower's spigot to an engine. The train yard stretched a quarter mile in every flat, featureless direction. Next to the water tower was a square courtyard stocked with twenty or thirty axles and rail wheels. A few yards beyond that were the outskirts of the large city. Ragged mountains broke through from behind the trees and buildings and dominated the eastern horizon.

"You mind if I have a look at one of your Thunderers?" Beau pointed at her Colts.

Abigail glanced down at her sidearms, paused for a beat then opened her mouth to reply.

"Here …" Sliding his revolver from its holster, he flipped it and held it out to her. "I'll let you see mine first."

Abigail smiled again and after another brief hesitation reached for the gun. Beau gently placed it in her hand. His dual-action, .41 caliber Colt Thunderer was identical to the pair she wore on her hips. The only difference was its aesthetics. Whereas her guns were nickel plated with gleaming, pearl handles, Beau's Colt had a dull, blued finish with polished ebony grips. On each side was a pearl inlay.

"Why skulls?" Abigail traced the inlays with her finger.

"More menacing I guess. Supposed to strike fear in everyday folk." Beau sat back and watched her. "It was given to me by my boss. He has a flair for the theatrical. I like it because I can fill the air with lead very quickly."

Abigail set it to half-cock, flipped open the loading gate and pulled the base-pin. Dropping the cylinder into her open palm, she sighted down the barrel. "It needs to be cleaned."

Beau sat up and raised an eyebrow. "I'm sure it does."

She shook the cylinder and emptied the six rounds into her hand. Holding one to the light, she examined it. "Did you modify these?"

"If you cut an 'X' into the lead ..." Sliding a knife from his boot, Beau mimed the action of pulling its blade across a bullet. "... it will expand when it hits its target and do more damage. Just something I learned a while back."

"Hmm." She reloaded the cylinder and reassembled the gun. Afterward she flipped it and handed it back to him.

As Beau opened the gate, spun the cylinder and checked that everything was correct, Abigail slid her right Colt from its holster.

"Guess I'd better show you mine." She flipped it and handed it over.

Beau accepted the gun and turned it in the light. She watched him disassemble her Colt with smooth, practiced precision.

"This is a beautiful weapon." He snapped the gun back together and ran his fingers over the polished barrel. "Seems appropriate a woman like you owns two of them." Beau handed it back.

Abigail smiled for a third time and holstered her revolver. As Beau turned and looked out the window at the empty train yard, she studied him. Though he only had a couple of inches on her his demeanor made him seem taller. His hair was nearly black and his skin was red from the sun. Dark brown eyes glistened in the high, noon sunlight. If his name wasn't obviously French, one might think he had Indian blood. He seemed to favor his right side and tried to hide the fact that his left shoulder was injured. She wondered if Cincinnati had done the damage to him.

"You think we'll find him in Blackwater?"

Beau turned his head and met her eyes. "No. I think we'll have to chase him all the way to Durango."

THIRTY-EIGHT

AS BECKETT WATCHED the marshal from the darkness of the alley, he pulled the Bowie tighter against the neck of one of the tall brothers who'd stopped the train. Greasy remnants of a meat pie dripped from the his chin onto the blade.

"What's his name?"

"Zebediah Cain," the tall man said through his teeth.

Becket jerked him backward out of the alley and around the corner into an empty blacksmith shop. "You gonna play by the rules?"

"Yes."

"And if you don't?"

"You'll pull that knife through my neck until my head flips backward."

"Exactly. Now, get to it."

"How can I be sure you won't kill me?"

"You can't." Beckett slowly dragged the blade across his throat, drawing blood.

"Alright, alright!"

Beckett paused for a moment and waited.

The tall man with the hawk-nose and the scar across his face cleared his throat and yelled. "Zeb, we got him!"

"Again," Beckett said into his ear.

"We got Valentine!" The man's voice echoed down the street.

As soon as the words left his mouth, Beckett removed the knife and slammed the man's head against a large anvil. He then dragged his limp body into the empty blacksmith building.

Beckett quickly returned to the front, crouched beside the outer wall and waited with his Bowie in hand. He could hear Marshal Zebediah Cain's footsteps advancing down the alley. When Beckett saw the tip of his boot, he sprung into action.

Keeping in a crouched stance, Beckett stepped around the corner and thrust his Bowie upwards toward Cain's head, aiming for the soft underside of his jaw.

In the last split second of the swing, Cain reacted and dodged to his left. Beckett's blade missed its target, grazed the marshal's cheek and severed his ear.

The momentum of Beckett's failed strike sent him into the alley where he spun and landed with his back to the south wall.

Cain tumbled to a knee against the north wall and clawed at the gaping bloody mess where his right ear had been. Before the marshal could turn and raise his revolver, Beckett lunged across the alley with an underhand swing of his Bowie.

Cain dropped to the dirt onto his right shoulder to avoid the attack and turned his gun toward Beckett as his knife struck the wall. The marshal's shot went off harmlessly into the sky and echoed through the alley.

Pushing backward, Beckett let go of his knife which was stuck in the wooden siding, took a step sideways and kicked Cain's gun from his hand. It slid to a stop in the dusty center of Harrison Street.

Before Beckett could regain his balance, Cain grabbed his right leg and pulled it out from under him. Beckett fell onto his wounded right flank and let out a howl. The immense pain paralyzed him for a moment then he rolled onto his front and pushed up onto his knees.

The marshal was on his feet before Beckett could react and swung his boot into his side. The impact cracked ribs and missed his wounds by just inches. A second kick landed dead center on his infected flank and sent him screaming onto his back.

Cain stepped back, panting. He touched the hole on the side of his head and looked at the blood on his hand. "You cut my *fucking* ear off!"

Beckett pushed off of the dirt. He looked down the alley to Main Street. The parade was still in full force. Apparently no one had heard Cain's gunshot over the drums.

Cain reached behind his back and found that his second revolver was missing. Beckett followed his eyes to Harrison street where an ivory-handled Colt gleamed in the sunlight. The marshal then touched the bloody remains of his ear.

"I'm a firm believer in an-eye-for-an-eye." Turning back to the north wall, he plucked Beckett's Bowie from the siding. "But I think we need to start with an ear-for-an-ear first."

As he stepped forward with the large knife in hand, Beckett swung his right leg and kicked Cain's feet out from under him. He fell onto his back and let out a breathy grunt. The Bowie landed tip-first in the dirt.

Beckett scrambled to his feet.

Cain struggled to catch his breath.

As Beckett snatched his Bowie and turned, he heard a voice yell from Harrison.

"Zeb?"

Becket recognized the short, hairy man riding from the south end of the street as the one who'd shot at the train's passengers after the explosion. Dried blood ran from his ears down his head and neck.

"Is that Valentine?" the hairy man yelled again. He pulled his revolver and fired.

The bullet missed Beckett by a foot and splintered the adjacent wall. He ducked and turned away.

"No, Sockeye." Cain rolled over and crawled toward his guns. "He's mine."

The hairy man slid from his horse and fired again. This time the bullet missed by just an inch.

Cain scrambled over to the man and grabbed him by his throat. "He's mine! Stop fucking shooting!"

"Holy shit, Zeb. What happened to your ear?"

As Cain pushed the hairy man aside and picked up his Merwin Hulbert, Beckett turned and stumbled down the alley. Grabbing his wounded flank, he picked up his pace and headed straight for the parade.

THIRTY-NINE

REUBEN KORRIGAN stood over the bench with his Colt drawn. Using the barrel of his Winchester he slowly lifted the sleeping man's hat. As the brim's shadow receded, Reuben saw a stubble-covered chin caked with what looked like dried vomit.

"Gus?" The voice came from across the street.

Reuben turned to see a middle-age shopkeep hurrying toward him.

"Whoa there, mister. I don't know what he said to you but he don't deserve to get shot." The shopkeep stopped just short of the sidewalk.

"You know this man?" Reuben gestured with his Colt.

"He's my brother. Had a bit too much to drink last night and he's sleeping it off. If he said something to offend you—"

With a quick movement of his Winchester, Reuben flipped the sleeping man's hat into the street. He looked like an older, worn-out version of the shopkeep. He was still snoring.

"Please, mister. I swear he ain't worth—"

Reuben lowered his rifle and holstered his Colt. "You happen to see a man ride into town about twenty minutes ago?"

"Ain't seen nor heard much with the parade and all. Been people comin' and goin' all week."

After sliding his Winchester into its saddle holster, Reuben mounted his white Arabian.

"Well, if you—"

A faint gunshot rang out through the buildings. It was barely audible over the clattering drums and cheering crowd one street over but it was definitely a gunshot.

Reuben quickly turned his horse and headed to an alley just north of his position. When he saw the woman in the chaps passing on the western sidewalk, he slowed and tipped his hat to her again. This time she answered with a coy smile.

Turning into the alley, he placed his hand on his Colt. Ahead was a line of people watching the parade with their backs to him. The drum and bugle corps marched down the center of Main Street followed by eight mounted calvary men. Another row of people lined the eastern sidewalk. The repeated crack of the rolling snare drums echoed between the buildings. Maybe he'd just imagined the sound of a gun. There was no sign of panic.

As he removed his hand from his Colt, Reuben heard another shot.

Then, a few moments later, he heard another.

Across the street in the far alley rose a cloud of black powder smoke. Reuben slid from his horse and drew his gun. He ran toward the wall of people that lined the west side of the street and pushed his way through.

The drum and bugle corps continued their playing as if nothing had happened. Bystanders across the street started to react to the gunfire. Some looked around in shock, others hurried north and south down Main Street.

Reuben stepped from the sidewalk to the dirt only a few feet from the drums. A bugler trumpeted the first few notes of "Yankee Doodle" into Reuben's ear. Flinching and turning away from the brash tone, he spotted a tall man with a beard stumbling into the street. The man held his right flank, looked over his shoulder to the smoky alley behind then collided with a marching drummer.

"It's Valentine!" The voice drew Rueben's attention to the alleyway just as Zeb reached the street with Sockeye close behind. Zeb made eye contact and pointed to the bearded man.

As Valentine pushed himself off of the toppled drummer, Reuben raised his gun.

A woman screamed from across the street. Then came two loud cracks from Sockeye's revolver.

The first shot destroyed the knee of the bugler closest to Valentine. A crimson spray painted his opposite leg and sent the him stumbling sideways into a group of bystanders. A young woman in a pale dress took the brunt of the man's fall. She let out a yelp as he crushed her with his weight.

The second shot hit the drummer closest to Reuben in the temple, blowing off the top of his head. Blood and brain matter coated Reuben's face. As he wiped it away he saw the drummer collapse like a dropped bag of sand. His snare drum hit the hard dirt with a loud, bell-like clang.

Instant chaos ensued. A cacophony of screams, yells and cries came from all directions. The calvary's horses reared and wailed. As one of the soldiers tried to regain control, his horse veered into the panicking crowd and trampled a small Chinaman. Hooves crushed bone and tore flesh as the animal tried to right itself.

While Reuben struggled to spot Valentine in the bedlam, he saw Sockeye fire two more shots from across the street. One ricocheted harmlessly. The other struck a fleeing old man in the back. His frail body fell to the ground with a soft thud.

"Stop fucking shooting! Valentine is *mine*." Zeb stumbled to Sockeye and cracked him across the skull with the protruding metal eyelet on the butt of his Merwin Hulbert. Sockeye toppled to the dirt as quickly as the old man had.

Gathering his senses, Reuben pushed through fleeing bodies and scanned the crowd. A few seconds later he saw the man they were after. Valentine was panting and had collapsed against a storefront on the west side of the street.

Reuben raised his Colt. As he thumbed the hammer, a young girl scampered from behind a building. She stopped and cried for her mother then turned and met Reuben's eyes. The girl wasn't more than five years old and stood directly in front of a crouching Valentine. There was no way to hit him without putting a bullet through her.

Reuben clenched the trigger. "Sorry kid."

"Drop the gun, mister." A stern voice called from above and behind. "Drop the fucking gun, now!"

Reuben hesitated a moment and watched as the young girl's tears streamed down and around her crimson cheeks. He could hear the clomp of the calvary's horses surrounding him.

"I will end you, sir!" The voice called again.

Reuben let out a long breath and dropped his gun to the ground. Holding his hands away from his body, he slowly turned to look down the long barrel of an angry first sergeant's Colt.

Across the street, two other soldiers were in the process of subduing Zeb. A corporal held a revolver on Reuben's boss while another forced him to the ground by racking him across the back of the knees with a rifle stock. Reuben saw for the first time that Zebediah's ear had been severed. Blood poured from the ragged hole.

Sockeye was out cold in the dirt. Another pair of soldiers rolled him onto his back and checked to see if he was alive. One looked back and gave a nod to his mounted superior.

There was no sign of Reuben's twin brother.

"Well now …" A man with a sheriff's badge halted his galloping horse and slid from his saddle next to the mounted first sergeant. He was older, had a bushy handlebar mustache and spoke with a thick southern accent. He looked at Reuben, Sockeye and Zeb in turn. "… It looks like you boys are in some serious shit."

FORTY

BECKETT COULD HARDLY BREATHE. Cain's boot had cracked multiple ribs making every breath torture. As he fell to his knees against the building's facade, he watched a frail old man take a bullet in the back just a few feet away. The old-timer's body arched unnaturally backwards with the force of the blow then crumpled to the ground as if he'd been made of paper.

Beckett knew that the marshal and his men were just about on top of him but his body had finally given up. He needed to rest.

As he pushed up and away from the building with his right arm, his ribs and his burning flank sent an explosion of pain through him. He fell back to his knees.

Maybe it was finally time to give up. Maybe it was time for the inevitable.

"Momma! Momma!" A tiny voice screeched.

Beckett turned his head to see a small girl slide to a stop next to him. She called out to her mother again. Then she focused her attention on a tall man pointing a revolver.

He was obviously the twin of the unconscious man in the blacksmith's shop. Same stature, same face, same hawk-like nose. The only major difference was that this brother was completely coherent and about to put a hole in a five-year-old to get to Beckett. He could see it in the twin's eyes.

Don't do it. Not her. Beckett couldn't get the words out. His lungs felt as if they were about to collapse. Closing his eyes, he forced a deep, agonizing breath. After letting it out, he pulled in another and allowed anger and rage to overtake his pain.

Pushing off of the wall, Beckett stood and reached for his Bowie. As he turned to protect the girl, he heard a revolver hit the dirt. The twin had dropped his ivory-handled Colt and surrendered to a cavalryman. Glancing around, Beckett saw that both Cain and the short, hairy man had been captured as well.

Across the street came a cry from a hysterical mother. Beckett took his hand off his Bowie, picked the girl up with his left arm and cradled her against his good side. Keeping his head low, he carried the child across the dusty expanse and delivered her to her mother.

"Phoebe!" The woman embraced her child. Tears ran down her cheeks. "My little Phoebe."

Burying her face into her mother's bosom, the girl sobbed. "Momma."

Beckett shielded himself with the brim of his hat from the army and the sheriff who had just joined them then stepped up onto the sidewalk. Placing his hand on the knob of the nearest door, he turned and stole a glance at Cain.

One of the calvary men had the marshal pinned to the dirt with a knee. A black pool of blood had formed in the dust below his severed ear. Their eyes met.

Without a single word, Zebediah Cain relayed the message, *I'm coming for you and I'm going to kill you.*

Beckett cracked a smile and pushed open the door.

FORTY-ONE

"**I'M SORRY, SIR.** We're closed for the day," a small, nervous man said, crouching behind a long counter. His tone was curt and shrill.

Closing the door behind him, Beckett stepped into the parlor of what looked like a modest inn. As he searched the room for another exit, the pain in his side resurfaced and he grabbed his flank.

The nervous innkeeper looked out the windows at the cavalry then stood cautiously. "Sir, we are closed!"

"You got a back door?"

"Listen, I'm going to have to ask you to leave. I told you we—"

Toppling to his left, Beckett fell against the counter. After a few shallow breaths he pushed back up.

"Are you shot?" There was more curiosity in the innkeeper's voice than concern.

As Beckett righted himself, he glanced at the wall behind the counter. The inn stocked a sundry of everyday items. A row of bottles to the right caught his attention.

"Give me one of them bottles of whiskey." Beckett reached into his pocket then slapped a coin down.

Taking a quick look at the ten dollar gold eagle, the innkeeper stepped behind the counter. "I'm afraid I don't have change for a coin of that value."

"Then don't give me change ..." Beckett winced and grit his teeth. "... just give me the bottle."

In one fluid movement the innkeeper snatched up the gold eagle, grabbed a bottle of rye and placed it on the counter.

"Now ..." Beckett popped the cork and took a long pull. "... where's that back door?"

***

BECKETT LOOKED BOTH WAYS before stepping out from the alley. The short, hairy man's horse milled around a few blocks to the north. Other than that, Harrison Street was deserted. Taking a long swig of whiskey, he hobbled across the dusty road and propped himself against the outside wall of the Blackwater Post Office. After another agonizing, deep breath, he took the first of many painful steps to the large Catholic church at the south end of the street.

"Hey!" A call came from behind. "Hey, you!"

Raising his slack right hand to his Bowie, Beckett turned his head. A smartly-dressed young man was hurrying in his direction.

"You alright?" The young man stopped a few feet away. He looked to be in his early twenties.

Beckett dropped his right hand and took a labored step. "Never better."

"I saw what you did back there for that little girl. You're a regular hero."

"I'm a lot of things, kid, but I definitely ain't no hero." He took another step and the young man followed.

"May I ask why that tall fellow had his gun on you?"

"You can ask." Stopping for a breath, Beckett popped the cork, took a swig and replaced it.

"Do you know him? Was he after you for some reason?"

Beckett continued down the sidewalk.

"Well?" The young man was persistent.

"Said you could ask. Didn't say I would answer."

"You staying here in town?"

"Nope." He took another step.

"Where you off to then?"

Beckett stopped and looked the young man in the eye. His pudgy face was greasy and blotched with acne.

"Jesus, kid. I'm off to get my horse." He popped the cork on his bottle. "That okay with you?"

"Why don't you have the town doc take a look at your side? Looks like you might have a broken rib."

After taking another swig, Beckett continued toward the church. "Don't need no doctor to tell me what I already know."

The young man watched Beckett stumble for another couple of yards. "You want me to get it for you?"

"Get what?"

"Your horse. At the rate you're going you'll be passed out drunk by the time you reach the Wells Fargo."

Beckett looked at the church a quarter-mile down Harrison. His side burned, his ribs screamed and his head was foggy with fever. He placed his back to the wall and slid down to sit on the sidewalk. "The stable next to the church. The saddled sorrel."

"Got it!" The young man hopped in place and clapped his hands "I'll be right back."

Beckett watched him trot down the street for a moment then tipped his head back against the building's siding and looked at the sky. As his sore and heavy eyes followed a circling hawk high above, he thought of the nine men who had stopped the train. Five of them were now dead and the rest were either out cold or in custody of the army. He may not have taken them all out but for being feverish and crippled, he was pretty pleased with the result of his efforts. Another slim smile crossed his lips as he let his heavy eyelids fall.

"Here you go."

The young man's voice startled Beckett. It seemed like he'd only just left. In his left hand were the reins of Beckett's sorrel. In his right was a small wooden box.

"Found this next to your horse." Looks like someone was rifling through it.

"Just slide it into my bag." Beckett pointed at the teardrop-shaped bag tied to the back of his saddle. When he remembered what it was half-full of he bolted forward. "Actually, just keep it. I ain't got no use for it anymore."

The young man shrugged and slid the box behind his back, into the waist of his pants. He then looped the reins around the nearest hitching post.

"You need some help getting up?"

"No." Beckett slowly and painfully pushed away from the wall with his left arm. "I'll be fine." The young man ignored him and raced over to help. He was careful to grab Beckett by his good side.

"Name's Jimmy, by the way. Jimmy Graves. My pa owns the town newspaper."

"Ah. I see." Beckett waved him off when he was on his feet. "Just lookin' for a good story."

"Always."

"Here." He handed over the half-empty bottle of whiskey. "Hold this for a second." Beckett stepped to the left side of his sorrel and reached up for the saddle horn.

"You want some help—"

Taking a quick breath and gritting his teeth, Beckett placed his left leg in the stirrup and threw his right leg over the sorrel. When he was seated in his saddle, he reached down for the bottle.

Jimmy Graves handed it back. "You're welcome to stay with me and my pa for a few nights if you need to. You seem like an interesting fellow. I'm sure he'd love to meet you."

Beckett looked down the street at the blacksmith's shop. The first twin—the one with the scar on his face and the grease on his chin—was stumbling out with his hand on his swollen, bloody head. He teetered for a moment then fell against the large anvil.

Turning his sorrel south, Beckett reached into his pocket. "I gotta get on the road." He flipped another gold eagle to Jimmy. "Thanks for the help."

"Can you at least tell me your name?"

The first twin stood and looked around frantically. When he saw Beckett, his eyes went wide. As he dove for the ivory-handled Colt that Cain had left in the street, a pair of cavalrymen tackled him from the alley. They pushed his face into the dirt and shackled his hands behind him.

Beckett looked down at the curious young man. "You say your pa runs the newspaper?"

"Sure does."

"Tell him you just met Duke Valentine."

FORTY-TWO

"I'M SORRY, FOLKS ..." The conductor waved his hand to get the passengers' attention. "... but this is the end of the line. We had an incident on the tracks just outside of town earlier today and the railroad has yet to clear it. There are wagons and coaches waiting outside the station to ferry you the remaining five miles to Blackwater."

"What kind of incident?" a man dressed in a pressed, banker's suit asked. "Was it Indians?"

"No. Nothing like that. Just a minor derailment—"

A chatter of shocked and anxious voices broke out and filled the train car.

The conductor waved his hands again. "Nothing to worry about, though. Just need to take a slight detour is all. On behalf of the Denver and Rio Grande Western Railroad, I thank you for your patience and your patronage."

Ignoring any further questions, the conductor pushed his way through the car and into the next.

Abigail turned to Beau who was now sitting next to her. There had only been a single bench seat available when they boarded in Grand Junction.

"A *minor* derailment?" She raised an eyebrow at him.

"Takes a lot to derail a train." Beau stood and carefully slid his ammo belts over his shoulders.

"I put pennies on the tracks outside of Helena when the railroad first came through. The trains would flatten them into little copper ovals." Abigail held her thumb and forefinger up to illustrate the size. "Was always afraid I'd derail one."

Beau attached his sawed-off to his back. "Takes a bit more than a penny."

***

"**JESUS, I GUESS,**" Abigail said from the back of her beautiful palomino. "Don't think a penny did that."

Dozens of men were in the process of dismantling the remains of what looked like a blackened freight car that was lying on its side next to the track. Shattered debris from another car was strewn about for at least fifty yards in each direction. Its metal wheel base lay upside down, nestled against a weathered old church. A passenger car farther down teetered cockeyed, half on and half off of the track.

"Blasting powder or dynamite." Robarge kicked his Appaloosa along side her. "Only things that could've done this. Must've been shipping it to the mines. Some idiot was probably smoking in the car."

On the south side of the tracks across from the church was a buckboard piled with four bodies. Each one had a pale sheet draped over it. An old man shoveled thick piles of earth into the wagon next to the corpses. When he bent over, picked up a severed arm and threw it on top, Robarge realized what he was collecting.

He looked back at Abigail who had her eyes on a buzzard perched atop the church steeple. "What do you think he's here for?"

"Probably here for lunch."

"I DON'T GIVE A DAMN about your jurisdiction, sheriff." The first sergeant removed his hat and placed his balled up fists on his hips. "They shot two of my men—army men—and that makes this an army matter."

"Like I said before, sergeant ..." Sheriff Callahan lit a cigar and puffed smoke into the air. "... your job is to keep the savages under control. My job is to uphold the law." He dropped the spent match into the dirt, nodded toward the jail and continued with his thick, southern drawl. "You and your men are as subject to the law as them boys in there."

"Me and my men *put* them in that goddamn jail!."

"And I'm much obliged. Been a bit tougher doing it by myself. All of my deputies are off looking for the fellas who held up and *blew* up the train outside of Emberville." He removed the cigar, rolled it between his fingers and let a ribbon of smoke engulf his head. "Think they'll get a kick out of the fact that the outlaws they're after are already in custody ... thanks to you and your men of course."

The first sergeant jammed his hat back onto his head and stomped in a circle. After completing three hundred sixty degrees, he huffed and crossed his arms.

"This ain't right, sheriff."

"Well, it's right in my book and around these parts ... that's the only thing that matters." Callahan turned and stepped into the jail. "If you've got a problem with that, you can take it up with the judge when he gets here next week."

As the sheriff closed the door he heard the sergeant cursing his name to his men. Taking off his hat, he placed it on top of a desk that was empty except for a candle in a cut-glass holder.

The Blackwater jail was large and plain. Across from the desk on the southern wall was a reinforced cupboard that housed the sheriff department's rifles, revolvers and ammunition. It also contained the weapons the calvary had taken from his detainees: five knives, one Spencer rifle, one '66 Winchester, one Remington revolver, two Scofield revolvers, two ivory-handled Colts and a beautiful Merwin Hulbert with pearl-inlayed snakewood grips. It was enough firepower to take down a whole town. The cupboard was secured by a large padlock whose only key hung on a chain around Sheriff Callahan's neck, sharing the honor with a larger key that opened the five iron-barred cells that lined the back wall.

The two brothers were in one of the cells, the small, hairy deaf man and the one with the severed ear were in another.

"How you boys feelin' today?" Sheriff Callahan stepped up to the cell where the twin brothers were sitting and blew a stream of smoke at them. "Pretty shitty I guess, huh? Well, I can't promise you much about your stay here but I will tell you that you'll get two solid meals a day and if you're lucky we'll toss out your piss buckets every couple of days."

He took a few paces to the next cell. The deaf man sat on the floor leaning against the far wall. His head was bloody and his eyes were closed. The one with the badge sat on the bench, held a rag to where his ear had been and stared forward.

"Now, if you're really lucky, that fine little woman from the mission will come down here and bring you coffee in the morning. They call her Matilda I think. Well, I tell ya, she's a real peach." Sheriff Callahan placed the cigar in the corner of his mouth, cupped his hands and motioned in front of his chest. "Got this pair of titties you wouldn't believe."

He turned and paced back to the twins. The one with the sideburns and the scar sat and cradled his bloody forehead. The clean-shaven brother stood with his hands in his pockets and watched every move Sheriff Callahan made.

"She really is something else. I wouldn't blame any of you boys for wanting to take care of some manly business after seeing a gal like her." He met the clean-shaven twin's eyes. "Just make sure you clean up after yourselves when you're done."

"We ain't the ones you should be after," the twin said through clenched teeth. "The man who—"

"Reuben!" The one with the badge snapped from the adjacent cell. "Drop it."

Callahan turned his attention back to the man with the severed ear.

"Drop what? If you ain't the ones I should be after ..." He leaned in closer. "... then who is? Saw the dumbshit in the corner there shoot two cavalry men with my own eyes. Saw this one point a gun at a little girl." Callahan shot a finger in the clean-shaven twin's direction. "Pretty sure he would've pulled the trigger too." Turning, the sheriff walked back to his desk, crossed his arms and sat against it. "And I've got more witnesses than I can count that say they saw you boys stop a train, blow it up then shoot at passengers as they fled for safety. So, like I said. If I ain't after you ... then who the fuck *am* I after?"

ABIGAIL WATCHED as Beau talked with one of the cavalrymen. She had no idea what the chevrons and insignias on their shoulders stood for but assumed the man he was talking to was their leader. After a few words, Beau pointed at a row of four horses that included a white Arabian and a shiny blue roan. Finally he turned his Appaloosa and sidled next to her.

"Seems they have Zebediah—my boss—locked up in the jail here." He gestured across the street.

"The one who put out the warrant for Valentine?"

Beau nodded. "The sergeant says that apparently he and his men blew up that train and shot some people here in town. Says the county sheriff has them in custody."

"Your boss? Isn't he a marshal?"

Beau shrugged. "Well, he *calls* himself a marshal."

Abigail furrowed her brow. "Then why would he do something like that?"

Chuckling, Beau removed his hat and ran his fingers through his hair. "You don't know my boss."

AFTER TYING OFF their horses, Robarge and Abigail stepped up to the door of the county sheriff's office. He reached for the knob and found it was locked. Looking back at Abigail, he raised his right hand and rapped on the door. A few moments later he heard a voice from inside.

"Who is it?"

"Sheriff, my name is Beau Robarge. I'm here to speak with the men you have in custody."

A metallic click came from the knob then the door cracked open. Above the open end of a double-barrel shotgun was a well-worn face.

"And who the hell is Beau Robarge?"

"I'm their lawyer."

FORTY-THREE

ZEBEDIAH PEELED THE RAG from his head and threw it to the floor as Robarge appeared in the doorway of the jail. At the sheriff's request he'd removed his gun belts, his holstered Colt and his sawed-off then handed them to someone outside. When Robarge had cleared the threshold, the sheriff closed the door, stepped back and pointed his shotgun.

"Hold your hands away from your pockets and stay a full arms-length from the cell." The sheriff backed against the front wall of the jail. "I'll stay back here so you can have your *privacy*." He said the last word in a mocking tone.

"Sheriff, I'd prefer you not be in the room while I discuss legal matters with my clients."

The sheriff let out a loud chuckle. "That's a good one!" He gestured toward the cells with his shotgun. "You got five minutes."

Robarge took a few paces forward. He stopped three feet from Zebediah who was now leaning against the bars.

"Jesus, Zeb. What happened to you?" Robarge eyed the bloody remains of Zebediah's ear. Then he looked around at Sockeye, Thaddeus and Reuben in turn. "What happened to *all* of you?"

"Valentine." Zebediah kept his voice low.

"Shit. He was here?"

"He blew up the train. We followed him here." Zebediah carefully touched the side of his head. "The army stopped us before I could finish him."

"Zeb, they think *you* blew up the train." Robarge's voice was an urgent whisper. "They told me you held it up and destroyed it. Said you shot people."

"You need to go after him." Zebediah placed his hand back on the bars. "He's injured. He won't get far."

"No, I've got to get you out of here. When the circuit court judge shows up here next week, he'll hang you for sure."

Zebediah clutched the bars until his knuckles turned white. He spoke through clenched teeth. "Go after Valentine! That's all that matters."

Robarge looked around the room then leaned in. "And bring him where? Here? You going to kill him from inside your cell?"

"I've got that taken care of."

"Oh, you've got it taken care of. Of course." His tone was sarcastic. "Zeb, you can't buy your way out of this one." He pointed to the front window. "And even if you could, there's a group of angry cavalrymen out there who will lynch you the second you leave that door. If you let me take care of it, I'll—"

"Walk out that door, get on your horse and get Valentine." Zebediah stepped away from the bars and sat on the bench.

Robarge stood with his mouth agape for a moment then shook his head. "Sheriff, I guess we're done here."

The sheriff stepped away from the wall and followed Robarge with his shotgun. Grasping the knob, Robarge swung the front door open, stepped outside and slammed it closed.

Through the window Zebediah watched as a beautiful young woman with auburn hair handed Robarge his guns.

"A LAWYER?" Abigail placed the ammo belts in Beau's outstretched hand. "I thought you were, well …" She handed him his holstered Colt. "… a gunman."

"My father was a lawyer." He buckled the belt around his waist. "And my brothers are lawyers. I went to school for it." Unholstering his Colt, he opened the loading gate and checked the rounds. "Learned enough to know I like guns better."

"So, how are you going to get them out of there?"

"I'm not." Beau stepped to his horse, put his foot in the stirrup and hopped on.

Abigail followed him. "What do you mean you're not?"

He looked to the west at the sun. There were only a couple of hours of daylight left. "I mean, I'm going after Valentine." He nodded toward her palomino. "And you're coming with me."

FORTY-FOUR

BECKETT THREW the empty whiskey bottle into a steep, rocky ravine. Five seconds later, he heard the echo of it shattering below. The sun had almost completely disappeared below the western horizon and darkness was quickly taking over. An hour earlier he'd entered a thick stand of trees that was a welcome change from the rolling, dusty expanse he'd covered since leaving Blackwater.

Whiskey seemed to have little effect on his cracked ribs and the jolt of each hoof-fall was pure torture. Up to this point the constant agony was enough to keep him awake but he could tell the whiskey and the fever would take over soon.

Reining his sorrel to a stop, Beckett slid from the saddle and stumbled against a large rock outcropping. He caught himself with his left arm and pushed back toward his horse. His legs felt like they had no bones in them, his vision was blurry and the world around him teetered to the left. Closing his eyes tightly, he shook his head and regained his balance.

For a moment he considered unsaddling his sorrel but when it took the majority of his strength to loop the reins around a thick shrub, he gave up the idea and lowered himself to the ground. As he crawled back to the rock wall, his vision spun to the left and his equilibrium followed.

Supporting his weight with his left arm, Beckett turned his head and retched into the dirt. As his stomach clenched and heaved, his cracked ribs screamed and his side burned. Sour bile spilled from his mouth and stung his nose. After clearing out what it could, his stomach calmed and the world around him settled.

When he finally reached the rock outcropping, he rolled onto his left side and put his back against it. Pinpricks of light blanketed the indigo sky. He watched them twinkle for a moment until they also started to spin. Squeezing his eyelids tight, he took a few quick, shallow breaths and waited. When he opened them, the stars were still again.

Reaching into the front pocket of his jacket, Beckett removed a folded piece of paper. After taking another couple of shallow breaths, he opened it and tried to focus on the words he'd written after the shootout in Temperance. The three-quarter moon shed just enough light for him to read his final message to his son, Daniel. He read the eight words over and over until darkness finally made it impossible.

Beckett refolded the piece of paper, held it against his heart and let tears fall from his eyes.

FORTY-FIVE

"YEAH, HE'S DEFINITELY slowing down." Robarge knelt near a small river and examined a group of hoof prints. Even in the waning daylight he could see them clearly stamped into the mud. "And he's not trying to hide his tracks."

"Maybe he figures he's in the clear." Abigail led her palomino ahead a few yards. "Maybe he thinks no one else is after him."

"Nah. Not this guy." Robarge wiped his hands on his chaps and stood. "I've been following him for nearly a week now. He was hiding his tracks before he knew *anyone* was after him."

"Didn't you say you shot him? He could be too injured to care about his tracks."

"Maybe." He looked into the wall of trees ahead. "Or he could be trying to lure us into an ambush. He's done it before." Robarge pointed into the stand of pines. "And that would be a perfect place for it. Especially after dark."

"So, what do we do?"

Returning to his Appaloosa, Robarge removed his saddlebag and threw it over his good shoulder. "We stop here for the night."

* * *

AFTER TENDING to her palomino, Abigail dropped her saddle next to Beau's on the gravel-covered riverbank and sat against it.

"How do we know he won't kill us while we sleep?"

"We'll take turns." He pulled a pocket watch from his shirt. "Switch off every three hours."

A sudden breeze cut across the rippling water and made the hair on her neck stand erect. She crossed her arms and held them under her breasts. "No fire either?"

"Nope." Beau reached into his saddlebag and removed a small, ornately-engraved, metal flask. He handed it to her. "Here. This will help."

Abigail grabbed it and unscrewed the top. "Thanks."

She took a swig of whiskey and looked up and down the river. The large, almost-full moon lit the world around them in a muted, blue glow. To the north the water snaked through and around the rolling, dusty hills they'd traveled that evening. To the south it disappeared into the thick strand of trees.

"Mind if I ask you somethin'?" She handed the flask back.

"Not at all." He took a swig.

"Why are you workin' for a man you don't respect?"

Beau chuckled. "Actually, I have the *utmost* respect for Zebediah. I just don't always agree with him."

"Why's he have a marshal badge if he ain't a real marshal?"

"I don't know. It's kind of like this gun I guess." He gestured to the skull inlay on his Colt. "The badge strikes fear into the men he's trying to control. He's always been a little over-the-top. His confidence is as much his strength as it is his weakness."

Abigail thought of Beckett and how he'd handled Cincinnati, Eli and two other men with just his knife. He'd told her that being intimidating was more important than being armed to the teeth. At the time she marveled at his strength and his confidence. With Cincinnati still out there she worried Beckett's confidence had ultimately been his end.

"Zebediah sounds a lot like someone I used to know." She picked up a pebble and tossed it into the river.

"Really?" Beau's eyebrows raised "Was he um ... a *close* acquaintance?"

Giving him a sideways glance, she threw another stone. "He was just a friend."

Beau took a swig. "And where's this friend now?"

"To be honest, I'm afraid he's at the bottom of a grave." She picked up a pebble and rolled it in her hand. "Think your pal, Valentine, might've killed him."

Beau looked into the trees. After a moment he turned to her. "Is that why you're after him? I mean, if you don't mind *me* asking."

Abigail dropped the pebble into her left palm. "No. I'm after him because he killed my father." She flicked it into the water.

Beau screwed the lid back on the flask. "Oh. I—"

"Hey! I didn't say I was done with that." Trying to keep her tone light, she reached across and swiped it back from him. "Don't know anyone who only takes one pull from a flask."

She caught him smiling in the moon glow and could tell he was relieved his question hadn't upset her.

"I knew you weren't a real bounty hunter." He leaned forward with his elbows on his knees. "You just aren't the killing type. You're too ..." He appeared to be searching for a word "You're too sweet."

"Alright, that's it." She stood and brushed off her chaps. "Get up."

"What for?"

"We're gonna see who's faster."

"Listen, just because you're fast with a gun, doesn't mean you're a—"

"Yeah, yeah, I've already heard that speech. Now, get up."

Beau sighed then pushed off the ground. Abigail stepped back a few paces and turned toward him.

"Alright, Back up a few yards down the bank." She motioned with her hand.

"This is pointless, Abigail. It won't prove—"

"What? You scared I'm gonna beat you? Well, if I'm as sweet and helpless as you say, then you ain't got nothing to worry about. Now, hands at your sides."

Rolling his eyes, Beau dropped his arms and spread his feet a shoulder-width apart.

Abigail adjusted her holsters and matched his position. Her hands hovered a foot away from each gun.

"Now, draw."

Beau opened his mouth to speak but Abigail cut him off.

"Draw!"

As Beau reached for his gun, Abigail drew both Colts and mimed firing.

"Bang! Bang!" She spun and holstered them. "You're dead."

Dropping his half-drawn gun back into its holster, Beau Robarge smiled and walked toward her. "You got me. I didn't stand a chance."

When he was only a few feet away she squinted and studied his eyes. A smirk crossed his face as he sat back down.

"You're faking it. You didn't even try."

"Maybe." He took another swig. "And maybe you're one of the fastest guns I've ever seen."

Swiping the flask from him, Abigail sat down. As she ran the exchange back in her head, Beau placed the pocket watch on the ground next to her.

"How about you take first watch?" He slid down onto his back and rolled onto his side. "I think you can handle it."

FORTY-SIX

ABIGAIL WOKE to the sound of horseshoes crunching gravel. As she rolled over and shielded her eyes from the low, morning sun, Beau led her palomino to her so that it cast a shadow across her face.

"I saddled her up for you. Thought you'd appreciate a few extra minutes of sleep."

Sitting up, Abigail ran fingers through her mussed hair to smooth it. "Thanks."

As she yawned, arched her back and stretched, she caught Beau's eyes glancing at her chest. He quickly looked away and handed the reins to her.

"We'd better get going. If Valentine *is* injured, we might be able to catch up to him. If he's planning an ambush …" Beau hopped into his saddle. "… well, I'd rather just get it over with."

After stretching one more time, Abigail checked her guns, put her boot in the stirrup and swung her leg over her palomino. "I don't suppose you made coffee."

Beau chuckled. "What are you talking about? Bounty hunters don't drink coffee."

A THOUSAND YESTERDAYS

***

ABIGAIL WAS STILL yawning an hour into their ride. Robarge had instructed her to keep pace a few yards to his left as he followed Valentine's more-than-obvious tracks. There was no strategic advantage to their formation and in many ways it made them a more visible target. But the farther they rode, the more Robarge was getting the impression that there was no ambush. The simple truth was that he liked to watch her ride and he couldn't do so if he was in front.

Her hips bounced in the saddle with every hoof fall as she steered her palomino through the trees. Robarge stole a long glance as she stretched again, arching her back and thrusting her chest forward. He couldn't help but fantasize about the buttons on her blouse giving way from the strain. He jerked his head away when she met his eyes.

"Beau!" Her voice was a whisper. She waved to get his attention.

Robarge turned his Appaloosa and sidled next to her.

"You still think he's planning an ambush?"

Shaking his head, Robarge pointed at Valentine's hoof prints. "No. It looks like he's slowing even more now. I bet if we pick up the pace, we'll be right on top of him."

"You think it's because you shot him?"

"Don't know. I'm pretty sure I winged him. If the wounds festered, he could be in pretty bad shape." Robarge reflexively touched his own shotgun wound.

"HE GOT YOU TOO, didn't he?" Abigail gestured to Beau's shoulder. "I know you've been favoring that arm."

"It was the man he was with. A black fella with a shotgun. Just a few pellets. Got them out, got it cleaned. It'll be fine."

Abigail furrowed her brow and tried to remember any black men in Temperance. The only one she could think of was a piano player at Doc Sherman's saloon. She couldn't imagine him having anything to do with Cincinnati.

"Actually haven't seen hide nor hair of him or the dog since we got off the train. Just Valentine."

What dog? Abigail was about to ask when Beau held up his hand and reined his Appaloosa to an abrupt stop. As he placed a finger against his lips, Abigail heard a horse snort somewhere up ahead.

Beau leaned in close. "Let's dismount. Head in along the edge of this ravine and follow his tracks. Go slow and keep your eyes open. I'll circle east around that rock outcropping and come at him from the south."

Abigail nodded and slid from her saddle. After they tied off their horses, Beau touched her shoulder.

"Be careful. This man is full of surprises."

Nodding again, Abigail watched as Beau hurried east into the trees.

They'd been following a steep rocky ravine on their right for the past half hour or so. When Abigail looked at the ground she could see hoof prints paralleling it toward where she heard the horse. Drawing her guns, she crouched and stepped along the hoof trail, keeping her senses alert.

As she neared the large rock outcropping, she heard the horse again and positioned herself behind the trunk of a large pine. Peeking around it, she saw the shuffling hooves of a chestnut-colored horse through the brush. There was no sign of Cincinnati.

Abigail took a deep breath and continued toward the animal. As she got closer, she realized she'd seen it before. The sorrel tied to a bush not ten feet from her had once been housed in her father's stable next to her own palomino. She took a few quick steps, holstered her left Colt and ran her hand over its flank. *Had Cincinnati killed Beckett and taken his sorrel?*

Before she could contemplate it, a figure caught her eye in an open expanse fifty feet away. A man wearing a sheepskin coat knelt in the dirt with his back to her. He appeared to be holding his hat and talking to someone.

Abigail drew her left Colt, took a few long paces toward the figure and pointed both guns.

"Stand up and put your hands where I can see them."

The man stopped talking but didn't move.

"Let me see your hands, goddamn it!"

Still no reaction.

"I know it's you, Cincinnati. Show me your—"

"Abby?"

The man's voice was raw and hoarse but she recognized it instantly. Lowering her guns she stepped toward him.

"… Beckett?"

The man didn't move. He just kept staring forward. As Abigail looped around to his right she saw an elk-horn Bowie knife on his hip and a scruffy beard on his face.

"Beckett!"

A surge of emotion pulsed through her and tears welled up in her eyes as she raced to him. Sliding on her knees, she holstered her Colts and clasped his face in her hands.

"I thought you were dead." She kissed his forehead and embraced him.

After a long moment she realized he hadn't raised his arms to hold her. Pushing herself back, she looked into his icy-blue eyes. They were distant and seemed to be staring straight through her. The skin on his face was gaunt and pale and small beads of sweat ran down his nose. She ran her hand through his thick hair. His forehead felt as if it were on fire.

"Abby, please don't leave me."

"Beckett, I'm right here. I just found you." She cradled his head against her chest. "I'm not going anywhere."

"Abigail?" Beau's voice called from behind the rock outcropping. "What are you doing?"

"Beau! It's alright. We were tracking the wrong man."

Beau Robarge neared them with his Colt drawn and pointed at Beckett. "What do you mean? That's Duke Valentine."

"No, Duke Valentine is a gunfighter. Beckett doesn't even carry a gun."

"Well, he sure as hell did when he shot Sheriff Cain and his sons. Saw their corpses with my own eyes. He even killed the sheriff's head deputy, Cincinnati. And there's no one on the planet faster than him. Well, I guess other than this asshole."

Abigail looked into Beckett's eyes. "You killed Cincinnati?"

Beckett didn't answer.

"Valentine here faced them down in the street and took them out one by one. Just an old-fashioned showdown with the meanest, deadliest gunfighter alive."

"Did you kill Cincinnati?" Abigail shook Beckett's shoulders.

Beckett remained silent.

"Why do you think Zebediah Cain wants him so bad? Valentine killed his father, his two brothers and the closest thing he ever had to a friend. Hell, if you don't believe me, check his right arm. Duke Valentine has a heart-shaped brand just below his elbow."

Abigail pushed Beckett away and grasped his arm. As she slid his sleeve back, a ragged scar in the shape of a heart appeared. Instantly she dropped it as if it had burned her. She stood and backed away.

"I don't know who you think he is …" Beau Robarge pointed his Colt at Beckett's head. "… but this man is one of the worst alive. If I wasn't worried about Zebediah coming after me, I'd put a bullet in this bastard's head right now just on principle." He took a step closer and leaned in. "How's that flank treating you, you son of a bitch?"

Beau Robarge shoved a heel into Beckett's right side and sent him into the dirt with an agonizing howl. After a moment, Beckett came to and met Abigail's eyes.

"Abby?" This time he wasn't looking through her. "Abby, is that you?"

"Don't you fucking talk to her, you—"

"Drop the gun, Beau." Abigail pointed her right Colt and wiped a tear from her eye.

Beau looked over at her with a confused expression.

"I mean it, Beau. Drop it."

"You've got to be kidding me."

"I can't let you take him. He ain't what you think. I don't care what you say."

"Abigail—"

"Please."

Letting out an exasperated sigh, Beau Robarge looked to the south then to the east as if searching for backup that would never come. When he turned back and met her eyes, she could see anger and frustration in them. She could almost feel it herself. Slowly, his gaze softened as he focused on her, his expression eased and his shoulders dropped.

"Please, Beau." Her voice was calm and smooth.

After a long moment he lowered his Colt and tossed it away.

"And the shotgun. Slowly."

He reached back, removed it from its holster and threw it next to the Colt.

"Now, turn 'round and walk forward."

After a few paces to the east, Abigail told him to stop.

Kneeling down, she whispered into Beckett's ear. "Can you get up?"

He nodded and let her help him off the ground.

"Here." She handed him one of her Colts and spoke loud enough for Beau Robarge to hear. "If he tries anything, shoot him."

Beckett teetered in place, the gun hung at his side.

Removing a pair of handcuffs from behind her belt, Abigail holstered her remaining Colt and approached Robarge.

"Put your hands behind your back."

When he did, she latched a cuff snuggly onto each wrist.

"I'm going to have to take your horse and your guns. I'll leave them at the next town we hit." She tossed the handcuff key into bushes near the rock outcropping. "The key shouldn't' be too hard to find after we leave." She leaned in closer "Beau, I really am sorry."

Beau Robarge didn't say a word.

FORTY-SEVEN

IT WAS EVENING when they reached the nearest town. She rode behind Beckett on his sorrel, her arms under his armpits, trying to prevent his slouching body from toppling over. After she'd cuffed Beau, Abigail helped Beckett onto his horse and they began their ride south. A few minutes in, Beckett blacked out and started to slide from his saddle toward her. Luckily, she had only been a few feet away on her palomino and was able to wake him and get him stabilized. Afterward, she decided it was best to cradle him from behind the rest of the way.

She followed the ravine's river south and tried to keep out of view of a nearby rail spur that paralleled it. Figuring it was the fastest route to civilization, she pushed Beckett's sorrel as hard and fast as she dared.

Beckett was burning up. She could feel it as she leaned against his damp back. Falling in and out of consciousness, the only words he spoke were in mumbles and grunts. She heard her name many times as well as her father's. Beckett also seemed to be having conversations with his son, Daniel, Doc Sherman and someone named Nat. Cincinnati's name came up often and apparently had been the major focus of his fever-driven dreams. At one point Beckett even reached for his absent Bowie—she'd removed it and placed it in his saddlebag for his safety—and tried to slash at a nonexistent figure in the distance.

As they neared the town of Cottonwood Creek, a wooden sign with a list of ordinances welcomed them. Steering Beckett's sorrel into an alley behind the nearest building, she carefully slid down and leaned him forward against the saddle horn. Fearing he'd topple over before she returned, Abigail used one of the reins to secure his hands around the horse's neck, pinning him to its back. She then looped the other over a tree limb, tied Beau's Appaloosa next to it and hurried around to the front door.

"I need a doctor!"

The man behind the desk of the post office looked up at her but didn't speak.

"Please, it's an emergency"

"Are you hurt, miss?"

"No, it's a friend. He's very ill. He needs a doctor."

"I'm sorry but Doc Owens is out on a call to Ironwood. Guess there was a pregnant woman about to pop." The man removed his glasses and looked her up and down. "Is there something I can do for you?"

"How far is Ironwood?"

"About thirty-five miles that-a-way." He pointed to the south. "You ain't gonna make it before dark."

"Shit." Abigail ran a hand over her face. "Is there anyone in town who can help me?"

"Nope. Not in town …"

She turned toward the door.

"... but Clarence Monahan out at the old Five-Star Ranch could probably help. He was a medic back in the war. Only about seven miles that direction." He pointed to the west.

Abigail nodded, turned and stepped out the door. A moment later she walked back inside and over to the man's desk.

"There's an Appaloosa tied out back. It belongs to this man ..." She picked up a pencil and jotted Beau Robarge's name on a scrap of paper. Pulling a fold of cash from her back pocket, she peeled off two dollars and placed them on the table. "This is for feed and boarding. And when he asks about me and my friend ... " She slipped a ten into the man's vest pocket. "... this is for telling him we rode straight through to Durango."

The man looked down at the folded bill in his pocket. "Should I tell him to expect you there?"

"No ..." She searched around the room and saw an address on a package. "... tell him we're on our way to Mexico."

***

THEY ARRIVED at the Five-Star Ranch a half hour later. Beckett hadn't mumbled a word since they'd left Cottonwood Creek. His sorrel was over-worked and tired. Abigail wished she could have given it a break by transferring to her tailing palomino but with Beckett out cold, she wouldn't have been able to move him.

A wooden sign adorned with cattle skulls hung above the entrance to the ranch. Leading a quarter-mile up to a large house was a well-traveled dirt road. Mountains and hills surrounded the building a few miles in each direction. The ranch land itself was flat and mostly featureless. A long stand of yellow-leafed aspen followed a creek that traversed its southern side.

Abigail kicked the sorrel to a gallop as she crossed under the sign. The horse complied but struggled with each step and panted heavily. When they finally reached the large, two-story ranch house, she reined the poor animal to a halt.

"Help!" She stayed in the saddle and held Beckett. "Someone, please!"

Almost instantly, the front door of the house opened and a tall, thick man with a shaved head and a shotgun stepped out onto the porch. He stood motionless and stared at them for a moment until a woman pushed past him from behind.

"Jesus, Clarence. Didn't you hear her? Put down that damn gun." Not waiting for a reply, the woman ran over to them and looked at Beckett.

"He's sick. I think he's been shot." Abigail ran her hand through his hair.

The woman turned to the man in the doorway. "Dammit, Clarence, get the hell over here. Now!"

The man huffed and propped his gun against the porch's railing. He stepped down to the dirt and hurried to join them.

The woman placed her hand on Abigail's wrist and looked into her eyes. "Why don't you hop down, miss. We've got him."

Making sure Beckett wasn't going to fall to the opposite side, Abigail slid from the saddle.

The man, who looked to be even taller than Beckett and maybe thirty pounds heavier, placed his left hand under Beckett's right armpit and eased him down. He then reached for his left armpit and pulled him off. Beckett's boot-heels hit the ground with a thud.

"Let's get him into the house," the man said, propping Beckett's limp body up from behind. "You two want to grab his legs?"

They carried him into the house and down a long hallway to a room with a large window that looked out onto the west side of the property. Carefully placing Beckett on a low, brass bed, Abigail and the woman stepped back and let the man go to work.

He tore open Beckett's bloody shirt and long underwear and carefully peeled them away from his right side.

"Get me a wash pail and start heating some water."

The woman turned and left the room. Abigail stepped around the bed and knelt on the opposite side.

"I think he has a fever." She ran her fingers softly over Beckett's forehead.

"Sure as hell does. These have been festering for a while." He carefully touched the reddened puncture wounds on Beckett's flank. "Looks like he got the lead out, though." He moved his hand to a large, colorful bruise above them. "Got some cracked ribs too. When was he shot?"

"I don't know. Just found him this morning." Abigail took Beckett's damp and languid hand. "Is he going to be okay?"

"Here you go." The woman returned with some rags and a porcelain wash basin full of water. She set it on a side table, dipped a rag into it and rung it out. "I've got some more heating on the stove." She handed the damp rag to Abigail. "Put this on his forehead."

Abigail obeyed, looking at Beckett's eyes as they moved beneath their pale lids.

"Miss, I think we should let Clarence work." The woman held out a hand. "Why don't we get you something to eat?"

Not wanting to leave Beckett's side, Abigail hesitated.

"Please, miss. Your being here won't help him."

After a long moment, Abigail leaned over, gave a delicate kiss to each of Beckett's dancing eyelids then stood. The woman reached over, took her arm and led her out the door.

FORTY-EIGHT

"**PLEASE, HAVE A SEAT** and rest. Poor thing, you look completely frazzled." The woman escorted Abigail into a large parlor at the front of the house and sat her down in the middle of a pink, floral sofa. "I'm going to deliver that hot water then I'll pour you some tea." She turned and entered the adjacent kitchen.

Abigail nodded and stared down the hall. She watched the woman carry a steaming kettle into Beckett's room then walk back up the hall and into to the kitchen. A moment later Abigail stood. "The horses. I need to tend to them."

The woman returned to the parlor with two small teacups. "Don't you worry about it. I had Rebecca set them up in our stables. She's probably brushing them down as we speak." She placed a cup on a polished, oval table in front of the sofa.

Abigail looked aimlessly out through the open front door then sat back down. The ranch house's entry was enormous. It's ceilings vaulted to the second floor where a balcony looked down on the room below. Wood-paneled walls were adorned with taxidermy animals of all kinds. A massive moose head was propped above a stone fireplace on the north side. Across from the sofa were two, ornately upholstered, high-backed chairs, each with its own side table. The woman sat in the one closest to the kitchen.

"Name's Molly. Molly Monahan ..." She turned and looked down the hall. "... the big fella seeing to your friend is my husband Clarence."

Abigail watched Molly as she took a drink from her steaming cup. She was small, thin and almost boyish in stature with wide shoulders but modest hips. A mess of gray-streaked dark hair was balled up into a bun on top of her perfectly oval head and a pair of thin-rimmed glasses sat across her tiny nose. She looked to be in her late fifties but seemed full of life and attitude, not unlike Abigail's own mother.

Molly raised one of her dark eyebrows. "I don't mind calling you 'Miss' but it might be more practical to know your name as well."

"I'm sorry. My name is Abigail."

"And your friend?"

Abigail looked back down the hall. "Beckett."

"Well, Miss Abigail, it's wonderful to meet you."

After a long moment and a sip of tea, Abigail looked back at Molly. "Thank you so much for takin' care of him. Don't know what I would've done otherwise."

"Happy to do it." Molly placed her cup on one of the side tables and sat back in her chair. "Clarence and I were a young couple in love once. I know how you feel."

Taken aback, Abigail stuttered. "Oh, it ain't ... I mean, we ain't ..." She took a deep breath and composed herself. "I mean, I barely know him ..."

"In my experience it doesn't take much."

Abigail stared down the hall.

"Saw how you were looking at him and just assumed." Molly picked up her cup and took a sip. "Didn't mean anything by it."

"Just never thought I'd see him again. I guess I—"

"Rebecca!" Molly stood and gestured to the front door. "Abigail, I would like you to meet our granddaughter, Rebecca."

Abigail turned to see a girl with golden hair and rosy cheeks standing in the doorway. She looked to be about nine or ten and tall for her age. Her pink dress matched the fabric of the two high-backed chairs and was covered in dirt.

"Got them horses all watered and brushed down, Nanna. Can I have a piece of rock candy now?"

"I don't know. Can you?"

Rebecca sighed. "*May* I have a piece of rock candy?"

Molly smiled. "Sure you can, dear. Make sure you wipe your hands before you reach into the jar."

"I will."

The young girl trotted off into the kitchen.

Molly leaned close. "Poor thing lost her mother last year." Her eyes dropped to the floor. "The sheriff a few counties over delivered her to us not long after Cynthia passed. Never knew who the father was. Some deadbeat cowboy I think."

Abigail's thoughts turned to her own parents, both of whom she'd lost within days of each other. With all that had happened, she'd never had a chance to mourn. Nor had she really accepted the fact that Garrett was gone. She'd been too busy focusing on killing a man who was already dead. Over the next few minutes, she ran the past week's events over in her mind.

Molly broke the silence. "Well, Miss Abigail, you and your friend—Beckett was it?—are more than welcome to stay here as long as you need. We have plenty of room and I myself would love the company. That is of course, if *you* were planning on sticking around …"

Watching Rebecca hum to herself and nibble on a stick of rock candy, Abigail looked around the warm, inviting home. She glanced at Molly who smiled and sipped her tea. Finally she looked down the hall at the room where Beckett lay.

"Can't think of anywhere I'd rather be."

FORTY-NINE

IT WAS TWO days before the woman from the mission came to deliver coffee to the jail. Reuben Korrigan tried to coax a word out of her each time she visited—which was usually once in the morning and once after supper—and over the next couple of days he'd used every bit of charm he could muster with no result. The chubby woman with the pale complexion just quietly filled their cups and acted as if she didn't speak his language. Finally, on the fifth day Reuben made a joke at the sheriff's expense that drew a slim smile from her lips. Seeing his opening, he leaned against the bars and spoke low.

"It's Matilda, right?"

She gave a slight nod.

"Matilda, how long have you worked at that mission."

Filling his cup with coffee, she glanced over at the sheriff who had his feet on his desk and was gazing at her. She met Reuben's eyes. "About six months."

"You enjoy the work?"

"I suppose."

Reuben looked into the adjacent cell. Zebediah pretended to be ignoring the conversation but nodded a subtle cue. He turned back to the woman.

"Listen, Matilda. We want to make a donation to your mission. A rather large donation."

Her eyes widened slightly but she didn't reply.

Reuben continued, "Big enough that if you decided the mission didn't need it … well, let's just say, a woman like yourself would be able to live the next few years in luxury."

She glanced back at the sheriff again.

"I ain't no whore," she said through her teeth.

"That's not what we're asking." He rolled his back against the bars, spoke from the corner of his mouth and nodded toward the sheriff. "All we're asking for are the keys from around that asshole's neck. Don't really care how you get them."

Matilda's mouth clenched shut and her gaze returned to the floor as she filled the rest of the cups. Reuben watched her for a long moment then gave an I-tried-my-best look to Zebediah. As he pushed away from the bars, he felt her presence behind him.

"Exactly how big of a donation are we talkin'?"

ROBARGE WALKED into the town of Cottonwood Creek exactly five days and two hours after Abigail had cuffed him and left with Valentine. It hadn't taken long to find the keys she'd tossed into the bushes and within minutes he was free of the cuffs. Not wishing to go back to

Blackwater to confront Zebediah and not wanting to deal with how he felt about a woman he'd only just met, he'd spent the first two days contemplating his next move. The next few were taken up by a long, uphill walk to the nearest civilization.

He was hungry, tired and desperately needed a drink. The first building he came to was the town post office. Stepping up to its porch, he pushed open the door. A man wearing a pair of wire-rim glasses was in the process of counting crates and checking off a tally sheet.

Robarge cleared his throat. "Excuse me. Could you tell me were I can find the livery?"

The man checked two more items then turned. "Down the street, second building from the end on the left. Can't miss it." He lowered his glasses. "You looking to buy a horse?"

Glancing down at himself, Robarge realized it was obvious he'd been walking for quite a while. "Looking to find mine. A woman was supposed to've left it here for me."

Placing his notes on his desk, the man pulled open a drawer and removed a piece of paper. "If you give me your name I might be able to help you."

"Robarge."

The man gave him a look as if he were waiting for more.

"First name's Beau. Listen, if you know—"

The man reached into his drawer and placed a ebony-handled Colt onto the desk. "Got your sawed-off shotgun here, too. Didn't want the sheriff askin' too many questions when I took your horse down to the livery. It's bein' cared for down there."

"You're telling me my Appaloosa is here"

"Down at the livery, yes."

The man picked up the Colt and looked at its inlay. "What's the skull for anyways? Was wonderin' that since I pulled it from your saddlebag."

Robarge swiped the gun from him, opened it, checked it and slid it into its holster. He then reached into the desk and grabbed his shotgun. Cracking it open, he checked that it was loaded, closed it and pointed the barrels at the man's forehead.

"Where is she?"

All color drained from the man's face. His jaw vibrated as he struggled with an answer. None came.

"Where is the woman who left my horse?"

"D-D-Durango."

"Bullshit!" Robarge pushed the barrels forward until they touched the man's skin. "Where is she?"

"Said to tell you she was goin' to Mexico. I swear that's all I know."

Robarge stared at him for five seconds then cocked both hammers. The metal clinked loudly in the large wooden room.

The man closed his eyes and pointed a shaky finger to the west. "She and whoever she's with are out at the Five-Star Ranch. S-s-seven miles that way."

The sound of liquid trickling onto the wood floor broke the silence followed by the smell of urine.

Robarge lowered his shotgun and slid it into its holster. "What do I owe you for the horse?"

Opening his eyes slowly, the man looked like he was about to topple over. "What?"

"For boarding my Appaloosa. What do I owe you?"

The man looked around the room as if shocked to see it. "Nothing. The woman took care of it."

Robarge turned toward the door. "Thanks for the information."

"You ain't goin' to hurt her are you?"

Stopping in the doorway, Robarge rubbed where the Abigail's handcuffs had cut into his wrists. After a long moment he continued down the street without a word.

FIFTY

BECKETT'S EYES OPENED slowly. The soreness around his eyelids and the burning behind them were gone. He tried to focus on a face across the room but his vision was a bright blur. As he squinted and waited for it to clear, he searched his body for pain. He felt nothing. It was almost as if he were suspended in a warm bath. His muscles were relaxed and the excruciating pain in his side had disappeared.

As his pupils adjusted to the light, he began to make out the face. Behind a large, flat nose was a mess of black hair. Rows of sharp teeth glistened in the figure's open mouth. Closing his eyes, he reached up with his left hand and rubbed them. When he looked again, he realized the face was that of a large black bear, its head mounted to a wooden plaque on a wall.

Running his palm down his face, he found that his cheeks had been recently shaved and his beard trimmed. As he turned his hand over he saw that its calloused skin had been cleaned and his nails scrubbed.

He lay in a wide bed under a white sheet and a multi-color, patchwork quilt, his head propped up against a mound of soft pillows. The room around him was adorned with a mix of floral-print furniture and taxidermy animals. To his left was a doorway that opened into a hall. A large window on the wall across from him, next to the bear's head, looked out onto an undulating valley surrounded by glowing, sunlit mountains. A lone oak sat in the center of the picturesque view, its leaves orange and its shadow long. A soft breeze pulled and pushed at its limbs.

To Beckett's right was a small table and an ornately upholstered, high-backed chair. Another quilt lay folded on its seat. A stained-glass vase that held two freshly cut wild flowers sat atop the table next to a glass of copper-hued water. Fine flecks of silica were suspended in the liquid leading Beckett to believe that it had come from a well. Despite its appearance, the sight of the water made him realize how dry his mouth was.

As he twisted to reach for it with his left hand, a strong sting from his right ribs cut through him. Pushing through the pain, he grabbed the glass and drank. Just as he was about to drain it, he heard heavy-souled footsteps outside in the hall. Before Beckett could search for a weapon, a large figure filled the doorway.

"Well, look who's up."

"Who are—"

"He's awake!" The large man turned and yelled out into the hall. He then returned his attention to Beckett. "Who am I? Hell, I've only told you twenty times." He leaned over and peered into Beckett's eyes. Pulling over a chair on

Beckett's left, he sat down. "My name's Clarence Monahan and you're Beckett. It's nice to meet you ... again."

Clarence was at least three inches taller than Beckett—making him a towering six foot six—and about thirty pounds heavier. His sunburned head was shaved clean and thick, bushy eyebrows dominated his angular face. Although he looked to be in his late fifties, his eyes showed a youthful glow.

"Where am—"

"You're in a room in a house on the Five-Star Ranch. My wife, Molly, and I run it along with our granddaughter Rebecca. You've been here for, let's see ..." He scratched his glossy head. "... well, I guess we're starting your sixth day. When you arrived you had multiple buck-shot contusions that had begun to fester along with a few cracked ribs. There was also a badly-stitched wound on your left shoulder that was struggling to heal. You were hallucinating and had a hefty fever that finally broke a few days ago.

"Since then, when you've been conscious, we've been feeding you and I've been giving you regular doses of laudanum to deal with the pain and to help you rest." Leaning forward he reached out and took Beckett's empty glass. "Your last dose was yesterday evening and should be wearing off soon, if it hasn't already, so try to limit your movements." Clarence leaned back in his chair. "That should just about cover all of your regular questions. Like I said, I've been over all of this with you before."

"You've been taking care of me for almost a week?" Beckett sat up. His side was beginning to ache.

"Me? Not really. I just come in and check on you every once in a while to make sure you're not dead." He nodded across the bed at the empty chair with the folded quilt. "*She's* been taking care of you. Hardly left your side. Kinda funny that the one time she's not doting over you is the time you wake up."

Beckett looked at the chair. "Who—"

"Beckett!" A familiar voice called from the doorway.

As he turned and saw a face he thought he'd never see again. Instantly the pain in his side disappeared.

"Abby?"

She took three quick steps then continued on her knees across the bed until she had him in her arms. As she pressed his cheek against her chest, he could feel her heart pounding behind her breasts. Combing her thin fingers through his tangled hair, her nails brushed against his scalp and sent a shiver down his spine. After a long moment, Beckett placed his hand on her thin waist and ran it up her back, pulling her closer.

"You're finally here." She was out of breath. "I can't believe it."

Grasping his shoulders, she leaned back and looked at him. Her auburn hair was casually tied up behind her head. A lone strand fell and curled beneath her jaw. Subtle freckles danced across sun-kissed cheeks and over the brim of her nose. As her soft lips parted into a wide smile, her big green eyes peered into his.

"Abby?" Beckett said again.

"Yes …" She chuckled. "… it's me. I'm right here."

As he closed his eyes tight, he felt her fingers on his face.

"Are you in pain?" There was genuine concern in her voice.

Beckett opened his eyes. He met hers and smiled.

"Just making sure I wasn't dreaming."

FIFTY-ONE

HE SAT ON A GRASSY SLOPE above the creek under a stand of aspen, their small, yellowing leaves chattering in the breeze. A beam of midmorning sunlight warmed his back. As Beckett raised a steaming cup of coffee to his lips, he watched as a young girl—who had introduced herself earlier as Rebecca—chased after a chicken in a sprawling field on the other side of the water.

"She's a sweet kid," Abby said from behind him. "Smart as can be, too." She sat on the grass next to him and held out a bowl of biscuits and gravy. "Don't worry, Molly made them. I had nothing to do with it."

Beckett smiled and took the bowl. He didn't offer a response.

"You gotta be hungry." She pulled her knees to her chest and wrapped her arms around them. "Ain't had nothing but broth and gruel for the past week."

As he grabbed a biscuit and dipped it in the creamy sauce, he looked over at Abby. She had replaced her dress with a thin white blouse and a pair of slacks that accentuated her curves. A thick, bear-skin vest covered her back and shoulders.

"Was that my bear?" He nodded to the vest.

She looked down. "Yeah. Took it with me when I left Idaho. Sewed it up on the train to Helena." Abby pulled her legs in tighter. "My mother was dead when I got there. An infection took her the same day Cincinnati shot my father. Kind of poetic if you think about it."

Beckett stopped chewing and watched her. Her eyes were dry and wide. She brushed an errant hair behind her ear and took in a deep breath. When she let it out, Beckett swallowed and spoke.

"How you holdin' up?"

She smiled slightly and shrugged. "Alright, I guess. Didn't really sink in until we got here. I've had plenty of time to work through it. Molly's been a big help."

Beckett turned away and took another bite. The biscuits were buttery and light, the gravy was thick and full of black pepper. With each bite his stomach begged for more.

Across the field, Rebecca pounced on the chicken. A moment later it wiggled free and darted away. She stood, wiped the dust from her clothes and took off after it.

"Are you really the man they call Duke Valentine?" Abby looked directly at him.

As he finished chewing, he watched Rebecca finally capture the bird. She held it up by its feet like a trophy.

"Yes." He swallowed. "My full name is Beckett Valentine. The boys on the range use to call me Duke."

"You as fast with a gun as they say?"

"Ain't seen no one faster." He put the half-finished bowl down and grabbed his coffee cup. "Present company included."

Abby turned away. She picked a small daisy from the slope and twisted it between her fingers.

"So, when you left, after you buried my father ..." Abby plucked white petals from the flower. "... you faced off with Cincinnati and gunned him down?"

"Yes."

"You do it for me?"

"No." Beckett took a sip. "I killed Eli and those other two for what they did to you. I killed the sheriff for what he did to the town. And I blew Cincinnati's head off for killing Frank."

Abby plucked the last petal and let a soft breeze take it. She spun the remaining, yellow heart of the flower in the sunlight.

"And the man that walked into a bar ten years ago and shot up a room full of people ... including your son ..."

"That was me."

Abby nodded.

They sat in silence for ten minutes. Beckett finished his coffee and his bowl of biscuits. The soft, morning breeze slowly intensified and brought in a wall of dark clouds from the west. Soon the sun was hidden behind them.

"There are a lot of people out there after you. Lawmen. Bounty hunters. You've got ten thousand dollars on your head."

"I know."

"Molly and Clarence asked if we would stay on and help out. Said they have plenty of room and plenty of work."

Beckett nodded.

"You don't have to keep running."

He turned and met her eyes. "I've got to see him, Abby. Just one last time. I've got to say my peace."

As she reached out and touched his face, a resigned smile crossed her lips.

"I know."

***

AS THEY LOADED up their horses, Beckett watched Clarence and Molly walk hand-in-hand to the stable toward them. He turned to Abby.

"You don't have to come with me."

She sighed and cocked her head. "Yes I do. You know that."

Clarence called across to him. "As your doctor, I would like to reiterate the fact that I don't——"

"You don't think I should be riding a horse." Beckett cut him off and threw his saddlebag over the back of his sorrel. "I'm fully aware of how you feel about it."

"Please, Beckett." Molly let go of her husband's hand and walked over to him. "I don't know what you think you need to accomplish but it can't possibly be important enough to risk your life. Abigail told us about the men who are after you…"

Beckett shot Abby a look. She ignored him.

Molly continued. "... it just isn't worth the risk. Not for you or for her."

After securing his tear-drop shaped bag, Beckett took Molly's hand and looked her in the eye.

"Thank you for everything you've done for me." He glanced up at Abby. "For us."

"Why do you have to leave?" Rebecca ran into the stable from the rear entrance and embraced Abby. "Why won't you stay?"

Abby knelt down and wiped the tears from the young girl's eyes. "We'll be back. I promise." She gave Rebecca a long hug. The child sobbed into her shoulder.

As Beckett watched them, a feeling of guilt overtook him. He choked it back as he hopped onto his sorrel.

"You know you're welcome here any time." Clarence sighed. "Just promise me you won't get yourself killed. I don't want the fact that I worked my ass off to keep you alive to be a complete waste."

"I'll try my best."

Beckett waited until Abby said her goodbyes and hugged Clarence and Molly in turn. When she mounted her palomino, Beckett kicked his sorrel out of the stable onto the long road east. A few minutes later they crossed beneath the large Five-Star Ranch sign on their way to Durango.

ROBARGE LOWERED his spyglass and viewed the two figures on horseback with his naked eye. As they crossed under the large wooden sign, he slowly crawled backward into the trees. Sixty seconds later he was on his Appaloosa, heading down the mountain.

FIFTY-TWO

HENRY McCANN RUBBED down the bar while he watched Edith Monroe use her hand to pleasure a grizzled old cowboy beneath a table in the far corner. When the man finished, he leaned back and called for a beer. As Henry reached for a glass, Edith stood, wiped her hand on her stained dress-skirt and greeted a miner at the next table.

After delivering a frothing mug of golden liquid to the relaxed cowboy, Henry returned to his station behind the cracked mahogany and thought about his worthless life. Next week would begin his tenth year tending bar at the Deadeye Saloon and he had despised every second of it. He hadn't left the town of Durango in over a decade and had finally accepted the fact that he most likely never would.

As the hinges of the batwings squeaked and two figures entered the saloon, Henry stretched his shoulders and prepared for the barrage of unhappiness that was his life.

"A bottle of rye and two glasses," a tall bearded man said as he slapped a gold eagle on the bar.

Henry looked at the coin then at the man. He wore a flat-brimmed hat and a flannel shirt with the sleeves rolled to his elbows. As he sat down, a beautiful, copper-haired woman took the stool next to him.

Taking the ten dollar coin, Henry turned and pulled the only bottle of rye whiskey they had from the shelf. As he placed two glasses on the bar and filled them, he saw something that made his heart stop. Below the man's rolled-up sleeve, on his right forearm was a brand in the shape of a heart.

AS BECKETT TOOK a sip of whiskey, the bartender's eyes went wide and he stumbled backward as if he'd been punched. Clutching the back counter, he inched his way toward the end of the bar and across the room to a chubby whore.

"You know him?" Abby pounded her shot and poured each of them another.

"No." He downed another glass. "But he must know me."

"Think he was here ten years ago?"

"Maybe."

She threw back another shot. "You don't need to do this, you know."

Beckett took a drink then poured and downed two more. He slammed the glass onto the bar. "Yes I do."

After a long moment, Beckett stood and walked to the front right corner of the room. Standing behind a round card-table, he looked at the rest of the saloon. In his mind's eye he could see the angry cowboy draw his gun. He could see the blood spray from his head and he could see his friends die around him.

Crossing the room, Beckett knelt near a table against the far wall. As he pushed it aside, a dark brown stain appeared on the wooden floor beneath it. Cupping his mouth, he looked away.

"We know it was you." A voice called from across the room. "We saw you kill that boy."

Beckett turned to see the chubby whore stand up. The bartender cowered behind her.

"God damn you!" She pointed and spat. "God damn you to hell!"

AFTER LEAVING the Deadeye Saloon, they turned and rode out of Durango the way they had come. Passing a small hardware store, Beckett leaned from his saddle and pulled a shovel from a barrel on the edge of its front porch. When the owner stomped out and informed him that the merchandise in the barrel was for sale, Beckett reached into a pocket and flipped him a golden coin.

Abigail rode beside him for over an hour as they followed a large, winding river north. Low, gray clouds blanketed the sky and the smell of impending snow was in the air. A cold, paralyzing breeze cut through her as they crossed a long, wooden bridge that spanned a steep, granite-walled gorge. Abigail tried not to look at the rushing, emerald-green water forty feet below. When they finally reached the eastern side, she let out the breath she wasn't aware she'd been holding.

A few minutes later, after passing through a small cluster of pines, Beckett slid from his sorrel and tied it to a low limb. Abigail followed his lead and stood next to her palomino.

"You can come with me if you want. If you don't ..." He grabbed the shovel. "... that's fine too."

Without hesitation, Abigail hurried to his side and grasped his arm. She laced the fingers of her right hand into his left and followed his lead into a clearing.

As the trees parted, a soft rise appeared before them, its grassy slope dotted with dandelions, their bright-yellow heads glowing in the muted light like stars in a sky of green. In the distance, a patchwork of red, orange and yellow trees blanketed a low valley. Sharp, rocky peaks dominated the horizon far beyond.

Sitting cockeyed at the hill's crest was a small, weather-worn, wooden headstone. As they neared it, Abigail could just barely make out its hand-carved, two letter inscription:

D. V.

"**DAMMIT, ZEB.** They're right on our tail." Reuben Korrigan hopped from his Arabian and followed his boss up to the worn batwings of a dilapidated, old saloon. "We don't have time for this."

Thaddeus Korrigan and Sockeye Smith reined their panting horses to a stop behind them.

"Zeb, they're gonna kill us." Thaddeus turned his sun-bleached black and looked down the narrow-gauge train tracks they'd followed into town. "We've got to keep movin'."

Ignoring his men, Zebediah Cain pushed his way into the Deadeye Saloon.

"I'm looking for Duke Valentine."

FIFTY-THREE

AFTER RIGHTING THE HEADSTONE and propping it up with a couple of large rocks, Beckett picked up the shovel and sunk its tip into the hard earth. He could feel Abby's presence behind him, no doubt wondering why he was digging up a grave. It didn't take long before he reached a hard surface with the large metal blade. The wooden thunk of the coffin reverberated through the shovel's handle. After a few more loads of earth, he threw it aside.

Reaching into the front pocket of his sheep-skin coat, Beckett removed the small, folded piece of paper. As he opened it, a few white flakes, each no larger than a pinhead, circled around him.

Beckett looked at the note he'd written to his son. The ink from his unsteady hand was blotched and uneven, a result of the beating he'd taken from Cincinnati and the sheriff's men. He smoothed the creases in the paper with his thumb and forefinger. After taking a deep breath, he read the words aloud.

"*When death comes calling ...*" He took another breath. "*... I will find you.*"

Falling to his knees, Beckett let a decade's worth of guilt, sadness and regret wash over him.

"... I will find you."

At first the tears came gradually. When he felt Abby at his side, her arms around him, he broke down completely.

***

SHE HELD HIM for what seemed like forever. Tiny snowflakes fell and swirled around them and a soft breeze whistled through the trees. When Beckett had finally composed himself, he looked into her beautiful green eyes.

"Thank you."

Abby didn't answer. She just wiped the tears from his face and smiled.

Turning back to the grave, Beckett looked into the whole he had dug. The bottom edge of Daniel's coffin was exposed about two feet down. Grabbing his Bowie, he pried at one of the rotting boards and lifted it. A small pair of worn shoes sat toe-up against the end of the wooden box. Beckett felt a ball in the back of his throat at the sight. Swallowing it, he folded the note, carefully placed it inside the box and laid the board back in place.

They rode in complete silence back to the long bridge. As they crossed, the rhythm of their horses' hoof-falls on its thick wood echoed through the granite-sided gorge below. When Beckett reached the western side, he reined his sorrel to a stop and waited for Abby to join him. Looking back, he noticed she was completely stiff and her eyes were closed tight. When her palomino stepped onto the hard rock, she let out a breath and opened them.

"Not too good with heights?"

She chuckled. "There's a whole lot of things I like better."

When she sidled next to him, he leaned on his saddle horn and looked at her.

"So ..."

Reining to a stop, she met his eyes and raised her eyebrows as if to say, "And ..."

"Where to now?"

Before she could answer, Beckett spotted something out of the corner of his eye. He held up his hand to get her attention and she followed his gaze south.

Four men on horseback rode at a gallop along the trail they had taken earlier. They disappeared behind a wall of trees only a half-mile away.

Beckett turned to Abby.

"It's them." He pointed up river. "Go. Get out of here."

"Beckett, I'm not going to leave you. I can—"

"This is my fight."

She shot a defiant glare at him. "And that makes it mine."

Beckett sighed. "Fine. Cover me from behind those trees." He gestured to the north along the edge of the gorge. "Just stay out of sight."

Leaning from her saddle, she grabbed him by the collar and pulled him close. She gave him a quick, soft kiss on the lips.

"Please stay alive." She turned her horse and kicked it to a gallop.

When Abby was safely out of sight, Beckett slid from his saddle and tied his sorrel to the bridge. Running his hand over its mane, he whispered into its ear.

"Take care of yourself, old friend."

As the the hoof-falls behind him became louder, Beckett turned and walked toward them. A moment later, Zebediah Cain and the three men he'd seen at the parade in Blackwater reined their horses to a stop around him.

"Well, well, well. Mister Valentine." Cain leaned forward. "Just the man I was looking for."

FIFTY-FOUR

"EVEN THOUGH WE ALL seem to know each other in one way or another, I don't think we've ever been properly introduced." Cain slid from his saddle and handed the reins to the small, hairy man. "This here is Hank Smith, we call him Sockeye. He's deaf because of your stunt back there with the train."

Beckett walked north along the edge of the gorge away from the bridge and his sorrel. Cain followed.

"Thaddeus Korrigan here has a cracked skull because of you." Cain looked up at the brother with the scar on his face. "Smacked him so hard against that anvil I think his eyes have gone crossed."

Reaching a point half-way between the bridge and the section of trees where Abby had hidden, Beckett stopped with his back six-feet from the ledge. He could hear the water rushing below.

"This here, is his brother Reuben." Cain walked past the twin who had pointed his gun at the small girl. He held a brass-fitted Winchester across his saddle. "Amazingly, Reuben is no worse for wear. Like the rest of us, he *did* spend five days in a jail cell because of you. So there is that."

Beckett placed the heel of his hand on his holstered Bowie and watched the men surround him in a semicircle. Cain stood a few yards from Beckett. Sockeye Smith was on horseback to his right and the Korrigan brothers halted their horses on his left.

"And then there's me. My name is Zebediah Cain. You blew up my brother Eli. You gunned down my brother Mordecai and my father, Walter. And somehow you outdrew my friend Cincinnati and gunned him down as well." He removed his hat and gestured to his severed ear. "And if that's not enough, there's this."

Zebediah placed his hat back on his head and turned toward his men. He nodded and they pulled their guns and pointed them at Beckett.

"What I'm trying to say, Mister Valentine, is that you've just given so much to us. " He turned back to Beckett. "I think it's time we give a little back."

"DROP THEM GUNS!" Abigail stepped out of the trees pointing her father's Henry rifle at the men. "I mean it."

The man who had called himself Zebediah turned to her. "And what do we have here?" He looked at Beckett. "Is she yours?"

When the man he'd called Sockeye moved his Remington toward her, she pulled the trigger. In a mist of red, his revolver went flying. His severed right thumb followed it.

Letting out a high-pitched scream, Sockeye dropped his reins and cradled his hand.

"Alright, who's next?" Abigail leveled the Henry at Zebediah.

She saw the smile cross his face before she felt the cold steel on her neck.

"Lower the rifle, Abigail." Beau Robarge said softly behind her.

She froze in shock and disbelief.

"*Please*," he said in a mocking tone as he pushed the gun harder.

Exhaling a frustrated breath, she let the barrel drop.

"Throw it aside."

After she tossed the rifle into the trees, Beau unholstered her left Colt and threw it. He then reached around her with his left hand, his arm brushing against her breast, and removed her right Colt. Beau threw it away as well.

"Robarge! What a wonderful surprise." Zebediah's eyes were beaming. "Have you met Mister Valentine, here?"

"We're acquainted."

"Perfect." Looking around, Zebediah clapped his hands. "Well, since we're all here, why don't we get started?"

WHEN ASKED if he'd seen an earless marshal and three other men, the bartender at the old saloon had pointed First Sergeant Colm Hutchens north. Leading a squad of ten cavalrymen, First Sergeant Hutchens followed a set of tracks along the Animas river. When he heard a faraway gunshot echoing through the valley, he pushed his horse harder.

FIFTY-FIVE

"AS A MATTER OF FACT, Mister Valentine, you and I have met before. Ten years ago and about ten miles that way, to be exact." Zebediah pointed toward Durango. "You may not remember because, as I recall, you were a bit preoccupied having just murdered your ten-year-old son. I was working as the town's deputy marshal when a three-man posse brought the dreaded Duke Valentine into my jail."

He searched Valentine's ice-blue eyes for a reaction. They stared back unflinching, his jaw set.

Zebediah continued. "You see, the reason I remember *you* was because you left me a reminder. Well, two reminders to be exact." He placed his hand on his left flank. "I still carry that piece of led you put in my side. Took me six months to recover from that souvenir. And then there's this." Holding up his right hand, Zebediah turned it to show off its ragged scar. "This one is a *daily* reminder. You know how they say, 'I knew it like the back of my hand?' Well …" He traced the scar with his left thumb. "… that's how well I know you. There's been a thousand yesterdays between you and me. And finally ..." He held out his arms. "... here we are."

From behind, Sockeye moaned and held his mangled hand. The snow that had started when they approached the bridge was beginning to thicken. A soft dusting wafted across the rocky ground between Zebediah and Valentine.

"So, along with this ..." He touched his missing ear. "... and well, everything else you've done to me and my family, I really do owe you a lot. So much so, I've been thinking about the best way to repay you. And since I know you as well as I know the back of my own hand, I think I've finally figured it out."

"Zeb, can we get on with it?" Reuben's tone was urgent. "They could be on us at any minute."

Zebediah took a breath and walked over to the brother on the white Arabian. In one quick move he reached for Reuben's belt and pulled him from his saddle onto the hard ground. He landed on his back with a hollow thud.

"Get up." Zebediah put his hands behind his back and returned to face Valentine.

After a long moment, Reuben Korrigan caught his breath and pushed himself off the ground. Zebediah could feel his angry eyes on him.

"Here's what I've decided. First we're going to have a good old-fashioned showdown. I'll give you the same chance my father and my friend Cincinnati gave you. This time the only difference is, *I* will beat you. Then, while you're on your way out, bleeding to death right there on that ridge, I'm going to have Robarge put a bullet in your pretty little friend's head." He nodded toward the girl. "And finally. While you two are both rotting in a grave, I'm going back to your precious town of Temperance and I am going to burn it to the ground. Not before, of course, I slice the throat of your little friend with your very own knife. If I recall, his name was Samuel, correct? Oh, and I promise you, his death will be very slow ..." Zebediah smiled. "... and very painful."

This time there was a reaction. Valentine grasped the handle of his Bowie and widened his stance. There was obvious fire behind his eyes.

"An-eye-for-an-eye. That's the only true justice." Zebediah slid the ivory-handled Colt from behind his back and held it in soft light. "Which brings me to this. Do you recognize this gun?"

Valentine didn't answer.

"It's the .45 caliber, Single Action Army Colt that Cincinnati carried." He held it to his good ear and thumbed the hammer—Click, Click, CLICK, CLICK—then let it back down. "But that's not why you should recognize it. I rode with Cincinnati for the better part of five years and this gun never left his side. I taught him to shoot it. He cherished it. He almost worshiped it but not because of me." He ran his fingers along its polished nickel barrel. "Cincinnati loved this gun because it had once belonged to a man he had come to idolize."

Zebediah saw a hint of realization behind Valentine's eyes.

"The night you gave me this and this ..." He held up his scarred hand. "... Lucas Kirkwood, a nineteen-year-old boy from Cincinnati, Ohio, pulled your gun from my desk and pointed it at you. From that day forward, this ivory-handled Colt never left his side. You made that boy what he was and then you killed him. And that's why I'm going to kill you now."

Valentine's eyes were unwavering. After a long moment, he slowly pulled his Bowie from its holster and dropped it to the rocky cliff. It hit with a loud clang and slid away from him toward the trees.

"Give it to me." Valentine held out his hand. "Give me my gun."

FIFTY-SIX

BECKETT HELD OUT HIS HAND and waited. Cain motioned with his head to the twin called Reuben and handed him the ivory-handled Colt.

"Give Valentine his gun."

Reuben Korrigan took the revolver, walked it to the edge of the gorge and placed it in Beckett's hand.

"Go ahead. I'll give you time to make sure it's in order," Cain said in a patient tone.

Beckett looked the gun over. Even after ten years, it still felt at home in his hand. As he traced the fracture on its left grip that had formed after he'd cracked it over a gambler's head, a sense of familiarity and power surged through him. In a quick practiced movement, Beckett set it at half cock, opened the loading gate and checked its six rounds. After spinning the cylinder, he closed the gate, lowered the hammer and slid it into his right pocket.

He looked over at Abby and met her green eyes. The man called Robarge had forced her to her knees and was now pushing her to the ground with the heel of his boot.

She lay on her chest with her right cheek against the granite. There was worry in her eyes.

"Oh-kay," Cain said in a singsongy tone. He placed his left foot forward and hovered his right hand a foot from his Merwin-Hulbert.

Beckett spread his feet and placed his hand over his Colt.

"Since my men already have their guns on you and your woman, I'm going to forgo a countdown and just let you draw first. It's your move, Duke Valentine."

As the snow intensified, Beckett examined his opponents. Just from seeing how Cain carried himself, Beckett knew he was the fastest draw, so he would be the first to go. Next would be Robarge. Not only had Beckett already seen what the man could do with his drawn sidearm, he also had his gun on Abby's head. Third would be the man on the sun-bleached black with the dual Scofields, followed by his brother on the ground with the holstered Colt. Finally, he'd put a bullet in the head of Sockeye Smith who'd shot the two calvary men and back-shot the old-timer in Blackwater.

Giving one last look at Abby, Beckett flexed the fingers on his right hand and and took a breath.

As Beckett reached for his Colt, an impact twisted him to his left. A moment later a searing pain shot through his left shoulder just above where Cincinnati had shot him. When he raised his gun he was hit in the back of the hand by another bullet. Dropping his ivory-handled Colt to the ground, he looked at his bloody right hand which now had a large hole in the center of it.

A THOUSAND YESTERDAYS

Beckett fell to his knees and looked at Zebediah Cain who held his smoking Merwin-Hulbert level with him.

"See, Mister Valentine. I told you I'd win. And seeing as I'm a man of my word ..." Cain nodded at Robarge.

Beau Robarge nodded back then leaned over. After whispering a few words into Abby's ear he stood and pointed his gun. She turned her head away before Beckett could meet her eyes.

Robarge pulled the trigger.

The explosion from his revolver echoed off of the granite and through the gorge below.

"No!" Beckett yelled.

As he fell to his right side, he reached for his Colt with his left hand. Zebediah stood over him and crushed his wrist with his boot.

"How about one more for the road?"

Zebediah Cain pulled the trigger of his ornately-engraved Merwin Hulbert and put a lead bullet deep in Beckett's left side.

"Zeb! They're here." Reuben Korrigan mounted his horse.

After looking over his shoulder to the south, Cain lifted his boot and placed its heel against Beckett's hip. "I'll see you in hell."

With a quick shove, Cain sent Beckett over the granite cliff.

The fall seemed to happen in slow motion. Beckett felt weightless as the rock wall passed on his right. Snowflakes circled around him and air whistled through his ears. The pain from the gunshot wounds disappeared as he closed his eyes.

When Beckett hit the water, the world went black.

FIFTY-SEVEN

BECKETT EMBRACED THE DARKNESS. A warmth flowed through him as his mind visited the people he'd cared about. There was no pain. It again felt as if he were suspended in a bath of warm water. When his thoughts settled on Abby, he went cold. How could he have let her die?

When he opened his eyes, a familiar sight welcomed him. Next to the mounted bear's head was the same large window he'd seen before. This time, instead of a golden field with a rustling tree, the valley was blanketed in white and snow fell heavily all around.

From the doorway to his left came a familiar call.

"He's awake!"

Clarence Monahan entered the room and sat at Beckett's side. "Don't try to move. Even with all that laudanum, I guarantee it won't feel good."

Beckett cleared his throat and croaked out a few words. "How did—"

"How did you get here?" Well, I think you'd better ask her that." Clarence nodded toward the doorway.

Standing with her hands clasped against her mouth was a beautiful young woman with auburn hair and green eyes. As she stepped toward the bed, a tear fell down her cheek.

"Am I dead?" Beckett tried to sit up.

"No." She sat on the bed and took his hand. "You definitely are not."

"You sure as hell should be though." Clarence sat back in his chair.

Beckett looked Abby in the eye. "But, Robarge—"

"When Beau Robarge leaned over, he told me to lay still no matter what." Abby pulled Beckett's hand to her chest. "He saved my life by putting a bullet in the ground next to me."

Beckett could feel her heart beating.

"How did I get here?"

"After the cavalry came and chased off Zebediah Cain and his men, I rode down to the river and found you. Clarence came by as I was pulling you out of the water."

Clarence Monahan leaned forward. "When Abigail told me your plans, I figured it might be a good time to go into Durango to pick up some chicken feed—you know, just in case. So after you two left here, I hitched up the buckboard and headed that way."

"After we loaded you up, we brought you here."

Beckett took a breath. His left shoulder was bandaged and sore, his left flank was in pain and his right hand felt on fire. Closing his eyes he turned away. When he opened them he saw his ivory-handled Colt on the table next to him.

"You had it clenched so tight in your hand I had to pry it out." Clarence gestured toward the weapon.

Beckett grit his teeth and sat up. He could feel both Abby and Clarence lean over to help. After waving them off he picked up the Colt, checked its load and saw it still only held its six rounds.

"Cain is going back to Temperance." He met Abby's eyes. "We have to stop him."

"So ..." She sat up and placed her hand on her two holstered Colts. "... what's the plan, Mister Valentine?"

THE FRONT DOOR of the Blackwater Press building swung open and a dusting of snow washed across Jimmy Graves' freshly-swept floor. It slammed shut as he turned to see who'd entered.

A tall man wearing all black removed his hat and dumped a pile of snow from its brim next to the door. He then removed his long coat, shook it out and tossed it over his father's printing press.

As Jimmy opened his mouth to protest, the stranger reached into his shirt pocket. He removed a tattered, old picture and held it up.

"I'm looking for this man. I was told he was here."

Jimmy looked at the photo. It was a younger version of a man he'd met four weeks earlier. His eyes then moved to the stranger who bore a striking resemblance.

"Duke Valentine?" Jimmy lay the broom against his father's desk. "He came through town over a month ago. I'm afraid he's long gone."

As the stranger slid the picture back into his pocket, Jimmy noticed a large revolver on his left hip. He turned and stepped toward the door.

"Do you know Mister Valentine?" Jimmy couldn't keep the curiosity from his voice.

The stranger reached for his coat. As he lifted and slid his right arm in, the sleeve on his left fell below his elbow revealing a heart-shaped brand. He looked over his shoulder at Jimmy.

"We're close."

EPILOGUE

AN ABNORMALLY WARM, spring breeze brushed across the valley as Beckett turned to face the six bottles lined along the Five-Star Ranch's westernmost fence. His face was clean-shaven and his hair cropped short under a new, black, flat-brimmed hat. A black vest covered his off-white shirt and worn boots peeked beneath his black pants. As he rolled up his sleeves, revealing his heart-shaped brand, he stretched the fingers on his right hand. Although the wound was completely healed, he had yet to gain a full range of movement from it.

His ivory-handled Colt was tied low to his right leg in a new, chestnut-colored holster. On his left hip was the fourteen-inch Bowie Abby had recovered after his fall. As he parted his legs and took a deep breath, he hovered his right hand over his revolver.

Beckett drew and hit the first bottle. Fanning through five more rounds, four more bottles fell from the fence.

As the black-powder smoke cleared, the sixth bottle stared back at him.

With a loud explosion, it flew into the air. After two more shots it shattered into a thousand pieces.

Beckett turned to see Abby holstering her two pearl-handled Colts. Smiling, she walked over to him.

"You ready?"

Beckett spun his gun and holstered it.

"Ready."

ACKNOWLEDGMENTS

I WOULD LIKE to thank my editor, Michael L. Johnson and my proofreader, L.M. Kildow for again helping me look like I know what I'm doing. I wouldn't be able to do any of this without either of you. I would also like to thank my grandfather, John Kildow, for his insight and help while fielding my calls about hypothetical medical situations and gunshot injuries. Finally, thanks to my wife, Linda, for allowing me to pursue yet another dream.

Mark Locke Creative

MATT PRESCOTT, a native of Seattle, has spent every summer of his life visiting family in beautiful Coeur d'Alene, Idaho and truly has a love for the area. It is because of this love and his passion for westerns that the *Temperance Trilogy* came to be. When he's not writing, Prescott teaches guitar lessons and runs a small business in the music industry. He now lives in Coeur d'Alene with his wife and daughter.

matt-prescott.com
instagram.com/Author_Matt_Prescott
facebook.com/MattPrescottAuthor
twitter.com/MPrescottAuthor

Made in the USA
Middletown, DE
30 December 2021